"We've got to make a run for it, Shad," he said. "Let's get over that rise yonder so we can see how they're heading. Maybe we can get out of the way before they get here."

They spurred up over the rise. Even before they reached the top Jameson could see the cloud of dust that rose into the plains sky. Then he saw the buffalo coming fast, directly toward them.

"Lord," Shad breathed, "must be ten thousand head."

"That way, Shad," Jameson shouted, pointing. "Maybe we can get past the edge of the herd before they run us down."

Jameson looked back once at this thundering black sea of buffalo that would pound horse and man to powder if ever they made a misstep, if ever they fell in the path of this living avalanche. He saw the bobbing black heads, the black eyes, the little streams of saliva that trailed from the mouths of the running animals. He could feel the fear that swept the buffalo, that kept them surging forward, and it became his own fear, swelling in his chest, choking off his breath.

BUFFALO WAGONS

by
Elmer Kelton

JOVE BOOKS, NEW YORK

BUFFALO WAGONS

A Jove Book / published by arrangement with
the author

PRINTING HISTORY
Ace / Charter edition published June 1981
Charter edition / September 1984
Jove edition / January 1988

ISBN: 0-515-09499-4

Jove Books are published by The Berkley Publishing Group,
200 Madison Avenue, New York, New York 10016.
The name "JOVE" and the "J" logo
are trademarks belonging to Jove Publications, Inc.
PRINTED IN THE UNITED STATES OF AMERICA

10   9   8   7   6   5   4   3   2   1

1

THE BUFFALO WERE gone.

Gage Jameson turned in his saddle atop a hill
where the grass cured and curled an autumn
brown. Squinting his blue eyes in the glare of the
prairie sun, he frowned at the company hide train
lumbering along far behind him, the six-yoke ox
teams hardly straining at the double wagons.

Three months out, supplies about gone, and not
enough hides to build a Sioux lodge.

Grimness touched Jameson's bearded, sun-
darkened face as he stepped down from the big bay
hunting horse and felt the drying grass crunch
beneath his heavy boots. He was a man in his
mid-thirties whose gray-touched hair and long
growth of wiry black beard made him look far
older. His wide-brimmed, grease-stained hat was
pulled low to shade his eyes.

Last year, down in that valley yonder, his
Sharps Big Fifty rifle had felled sixty-two buffalo
in one stand, so many that the Miles and Posey

skinners had had to return the second day to finish taking the hides.

Now, with the first autumn weeks of 1873 slipping by, it had been ten days since he had sighted that last shaggy old bull. He had lifted his rifle for the kill, then had lowered it and ridden away, leaving the aged beast to graze alone on the short buffalo grass where once they had grazed in numbers so large that no man could count them.

What was one hide? One hide, when long stinking ricks of them piled up at Dodge City, awaiting shipment on the Santa Fe. No man could guess at the number. But this Jameson knew: the great Arkansas River herd was gone, like the Republican herd before it. Next spring the melting snows would bare carcasses by the hundreds of thousands scattered all over these Kansas plains.

A graveyard, it would be. A vast graveyard of gleaming white bones.

A blur of movement on another hill caused Jameson to jerk around, his hide-tough hand tightening instinctively on the sixteen-pound Sharps he carried.

He eased then, recognizing the sorrel horse Nathan Messick rode. Messick was his chief skinner and hide handler, and now and again he helped Jameson search out the buffalo. Rail-thin and gangling, Messick stood like a telegraph pole in his stirrups, waving his hat in long grand sweeps.

He's found buffalo, Jameson thought, a stir of excitement in him. There had been a time when it took a big herd to excite him. Of late, it was a great satisfaction to find fifteen or twenty head. He remounted and crossed the open, brushless valley in a long trot, the brown grass rustling underfoot. In places it reached to the bay horse's knees.

Climbing the hill, he found Messick still sitting there gravely waiting for him, his narrow shoulders slumped. An emptiness settled in Jameson as he read Messick's solemn eyes. "I thought you'd found buffalo."

Messick grunted. "Not exactly. I just wanted you to come look."

Messick reined his horse around and moved off the slope, his long shanks raised a little to heel the sorrel's ribs. Jameson trailed him, content in his weariness to move at a casual pace. Still young enough as years went, he no longer possessed the drive he used to have. Youth was slipping away from him, he knew. The frontier took it out of a man. The frontier and the war.

"There it is," Messick said somberly.

Scattered over several hundred yards of ground lay the bloated carcasses of some twenty skinned buffalo, now so rank that Jameson's horse snorted and shied away. Someone had shot them from running horses like a bunch of sport-crazy excursionists, instead of picking them off slow and easy from a quiet stand the way any sensible hide hunter would do.

"Tenderfeet," Jameson said harshly. "Even ruined half the hides, getting them off."

It had always bothered him, the awesome waste that attended the work of even the best hide hunters. Now he was galled at this senseless destruction which came at a time when the buffalo were getting to be so precious few.

"Hunters like that," Messick said slowly, "there ought to be a law against them. Spoil it for them that *does* know how."

Jameson shook his head. "Blame the money panic. They're hungry back East—no jobs, no food. And the railroad letting its construction crews go. They're swarming out here like flies. Anybody who can get his hands on a gun and a horse wants to hunt buffalo."

He saw something move, out by the most distant carcasses. His eyes cut questioningly to Messick's, and Messick said, "Buffalo cow. They shot her but let her get away."

"Why didn't you put her out of her misery?"

"I'll help you find them, and I'll skin them afterwards. But I ain't shootin' no buffalo."

Jameson rode to her. The gaunt cow moved painfully, dragging a shattered hind leg. Her bag was swollen and fevered with spoiled milk. One of those big bloated calves must have been hers. She was slowly dying on her feet, waiting for the gray wolves to come and drag her down.

Jameson stepped from the saddle and lifted the Big Fifty. Its octagonal barrel was thick and heavy and hard to hold true, but at this range it couldn't miss. The deep roar rolled back to him in the chill air. He ejected the hot cartridge case, let it lie on the ground a moment to cool, then shoved it back into his coat pocket to reload later. His nose pinched at the sharp smell of gunpowder.

"Tenderfeet," he said again, angrily.

He well remembered the awe which had held

him spellbound years ago, when he had sighted his first herd of buffalo. He had been only a kid then, before the war. The buffalo had been one rippling blanket of black and brown, moving slowly across the land before him, the front of the herd lost in the dust of the northern horizon, the end of it still far out of sight to the south. The rumble of their tread, the rattle of dewclaws, had gone on and on for more than a day.

And he remembered how old Shad Blankenship had snorted at him in '68, when Jameson had asked how long it might take to kill out the buffalo.

"By Judas Priest, young'un, there'll always be buffalo. Ten thousand hunters and the U.S. Cavalry couldn't get more than the natural increase, one year to the next. Kill all the buffalo? Boy, you're talkin' out of your head."

Now here it was—one old bull, one crippled cow, for ten days' ride. And these bloated, wasted carcasses.

Suddenly Jameson was weary of it, weary of the endless, hopeless hunt, weary of stench and sweat and caked dirt and disappointment, weary of scratching at the lice it seemed a man could never get rid of while he hunted the buffalo.

He drew the straight-edged ripping knife from his belt and knelt beside the cow, starting to slit the hide up the belly while fat ticks crawled for cover in the thick dirty hair.

"We'll salvage this one, at least," he said, his voice brittle. "Then we're going. I've had me a bellyful."

"Where to, Gage?"

"Back to Dodge City. The Arkansas herd is finished."

Dodge City, said the sign at the new frame depot. But everybody here just called it Dodge, for it was hard to use the word "city" and not smile doing it.

Dodge wasn't much to look at, a raw-looking, raw-smelling town of lumber shacks and dugouts and soddies and dirty tents, and a row of one-story frame business houses fronting each side of the shiny new railroad tracks. On down the way yonder extended sod corrals and a long row of hide stacks that you could smell almost as far as you could see, when the weather was a little warm and the wind from the wrong direction.

Something else was growing now: great piles of white buffalo bones, waiting to be shipped East for fertilizer and bone china and Lord knew what else.

Last year the railroad construction gangs had found Dodge already a bustling little village, huddled up on the north bank of the Arkansas River, halfway between Missouri and Santa Fe. It had started out as a whisky camp for the soldiers at Fort Dodge, five miles to the east. Then the buffalo hunters had located there, and for a while they called it Buffalo City. By the time the railroad came, there were by actual count one general store, three dance halls and six saloons.

But to a buffalo hunter coming in after three months out on the prairie, the town was as pretty as a new bride. Didn't matter whether the lumber was painted or not, long as the ladies were. Nobody complained if dirt trickled down from sod roofs and got matted in a man's hair or fell into his collar and went gritty there. At least there *were* roofs.

Who was going to be bothered if the bar was nothing more than a raw buffalo hide stretched across a framework of poles? Who would holler if the whisky was maybe pure alcohol with a little coffee coloring, or even that tobacco- and pepper-treated contraband stuff that some of the guttier ones slipped off and traded to the Indians? It tasted as good as French wine if you'd been out on the buffalo range for months. And by the time you started getting critical, you ought to be dragging it back to the prairie anyhow.

Two miles out, Jameson's crew came upon an old man in tattered clothes and dry-split leather shoes pitching buffalo bones into a wire-patched wagon that threatened to fall down and die right there. A layer of white dust clung to him from these chalky bones that still had a peculiar stench of death even after the months of bleaching in the sun.

This, the bone picking, was the last grim harvest.

Some of the wagon crew hadn't smiled, hadn't spoken a civil word in three weeks, for they were being paid by the hide, and the hides were mighty few. Now, as Dodge finally showed up ahead of them, a yell burst from dry throats. A fair sight she was.

Jameson grinned, though it came near to cracking his wind-dried lips. He wasn't a hard-drinking man, but like the others he found pleasure in the thought of bellying up to one of those flint-hide bars. The change, if nothing else.

Nathan Messick rode up beside him and pointed. Worry was in his eyes. It always was.

"Ever see so many outfits camped? Scattered to kingdom come, all over the edge of town and up and down the river."

"Poor hunting, Nathan. Out of supplies, sick of hunting and not finding anything. Maybe getting a little worried about the Indians."

"They could be out picking bones. There's a million of them."

Jameson shrugged. "Pride, I reckon. *I* wouldn't want to do it. Would you?"

"Nope, I reckon not."

Rough-looking men lounged in scattered camps, hunkering over fires for lack of anything better to occupy their time. They had gathered here in town, waiting, not knowing what they were waiting for, not knowing what else to do. As the Miles and Posey wagons drew close, the men would walk out and gaze curiously at the hides Jameson was bringing in.

Ahead of him Gage saw a familiar figure standing in a camp, and he smiled broadly. The old man's back was turned to him, but he would recognize Shad Blankenship if he found his hide in a tanyard.

Shad was an old-time mountain man. He had drifted up the Missouri and dodged Sioux and Blackfeet way back in the days of the beaver trade. And although white men often skinned him, no Indian had ever laid a hand on Shad's thick growth of rust-red hair.

"Nathan," Jameson said, "take them on to the Miles and Posey yards. I'll be along directly, after

I chew the fat with Shad a little."

Shirt sleeves rolled up halfway to the elbow and sweat soaking his old hickory shirt, the old hunter had put a wagon jack under the axle of one of his three hide wagons and was taking the wheel off to tar the hub. At the call of his name he turned quickly, his blackened hand raised in greeting, his red-bearded old face broken with a grin.

"Hya-a-a there, young'un." As far as Shad was concerned, Gage Jameson was a young'un and always would be. Shad had picked him up as a half-starved runaway kid back there twenty years ago, nursemaided him along, wiped his nose for him, and made a frontiersman out of him.

Shad's big shaggy black dog came trotting out, growling deep in its throat, Blackfoot-mean, until it caught Jameson's scent. The growl stopped. It wagged its tail in recognition.

Jameson stepped down out of the saddle and patted the dog's head. "Hi there, Ripper. You catching enough rabbits to keep that old musk hog fed?"

Blankenship walked out, grinning. "I don't need no dog to feed me, young'un. I'm still a better hunter than you'll ever be, and don't you forget it."

He shoved his big hand forward, then drew it back quickly.

"Forgot about that tar. Wouldn't want to muss up a hide skinner's clean hands." There was a shade of irony in the way he said that. He wiped the hands on his trousers, already so black that a little extra wouldn't be noticed.

"Them your wagons going yonder?" he asked,

then nodded his own answer. His grin was gone. Jameson could see that Shad hadn't done much grinning lately, either.

"You done as well as any of them, I reckon. A heap sight better than *I* done."

Looking closer now, Jameson could see worry clouded deep in the pale blue eyes. It was the same discouragement he'd seen in all the faces that had come out to watch his wagons pass.

Shad Blankenship motioned apologetically to the wagon he was working on. "Them wheels don't really need any tar. It's oozing out all over. But heck, what else is there for a man to do? He'd go crazy sittin' here waitin' for the buffalo to come back."

Jameson frowned. "You really think they'll come back, Shad?"

The old man shrugged gloomily and turned back to the wagon. He started to lift the wheel into place again. Jameson got hold of it with him and fitted it onto the hub. Shad faced him then, and his eyes held a hopelessness.

"They ain't, Gage, they ain't. They're gone, and we'll never see things again the way they was. Wish sometimes I'd died back yonder while things was the way they used to be. Wish I'd never seen the way the country's been ruined."

Jameson put his hand gently on the hunter's thin shoulder. "Come on into town directly and I'll buy you a drink. We'll talk about old times."

Shad's eyes were bleak and pinched in the corners.

"Ain't the town she used to be, Gage. New bunch has taken over. There's every kind of riffraff in there now, just waitin' to see if you got any money on you. There's some will cut your guts out with a dull knife or strangle you with a leather cord. And if the cutthroats don't get it, them crooked gamblers will.''

Jameson thought he knew what the trouble was. No matter how many months old Shad had worked for it, or what he'd had to go through, when he got his big chapped hands on a roll of money he was drawn to the poker tables like a fly to a freshly skinned buffalo. Likely as not they'd taken him the first night he hit town. Lucky he hadn't lost his wagons, to boot.

Shad shook a crooked finger at Jameson. It had been broken in some trading-post brawl long since forgotten.

''You tell them men of yours they better watch out for theirselves. Quick as they get paid off, there'll be a dozen wolves around to pick their bones.''

''I'll tell them.''

He had long wondered why an old frontiersman like Shad, wily and sure as a fox out on the prairie, should forever be so improvident when he came to town. He had made a couple or three fortunes in his time, and they had all gone the same way. He would never accumulate anything of value and hang onto it if he lived to be a hundred and six.

Shad frowned darkly. ''I been thinkin,' Gage. Thinkin' about going East to Missouri and taking up farming.''

Jameson blinked in surprise. Shad added quickly, ''I growed up on a farm in Tennessee, don't you know that? Had me a right smart reputa-

11

tion. Wasn't no young'un there could plow a straighter furrow or get more work out of a pair of mules. But the place just naturally got a little too small for me and my Paw both. So when I decided I couldn't whup him, I took my old squirrel gun and lit out.''

Jameson smiled and shook his head. ''You'll never do it, Shad. Maybe there was a time you could've gone back, but you'll never do it now.''

''You don't think so?'' Old Shad narrowed his eyes and poked his finger at Gage. ''I get the chance, young'un, I'll show you. You just wait.''

Jameson caught up to his hide wagons just before they reached the Miles and Posey yards. The partners leased from the Santa Fe a long stretch of ground adjacent to the tracks, where the hides could be loaded directly onto the cars with a minimum of extra handling.

The hide stacks Jameson had seen here the last time were greatly diminished, but the smell of them was about as strong as ever. He watched some of the yard crew toss hides onto a press and squeeze them down into a tight bale to be shipped. Down at the lower end a huge rick of buffalo bones was steadily growing. Miles and Posey was branching out.

C. T. Posey stood in front of the unpainted frame office, chewing a dead cigar and frowning thoughtfully at a short load of hides in a sagging old wagon.

Jameson reined up and waited, grinning. That was Posey, all right. He handled them by the tens of thousands, but he could still enjoy haggling with a hunter over fifty or sixty common cowhides.

Trying not to be obvious about it, the man on the

wagon was showing Posey the hides with the hair
side up. And seeing right through him, Posey was
turning them over to the flesh side, one by one, so
he could tell how many bullet holes, peg holes and
knife slashes were in them.

Posey saw Jameson and nodded a greeting, then
went back to his trade. He studied a moment,
wrote a figure on a piece of paper, then showed it
to the hunter. The man shook his head deter-
minedly. Posey shrugged and started toward the
office. The hunter ruefully called him back. Posey
nodded and did some figures on the paper. Then he
wrote out a check and handed it to the hunter. The
hunter, grinning now, climbed on his wagon, flipped the reins and headed for the end of the hide
stack where some of the yard crew would unload
him.

It was an old stunt of Posey's to beat the price
down as far as it would go, then give the seller a
few extra dollars on the check to bring it up to
some nice round figure. Always left the man smiling, out-traded or not. He'd be back someday with
another load.

Posey strode up and shook Jameson's hand, a
genuine gladness in what could be the deadest
poker face in town when necessary.

"Mighty pleased to see you, Gage."

"You may not be when you look at my wagons."

Posey stood back and surveyed Jameson's in-
coming hide train, his hands shoved deep in his
pockets. He chewed heavily on the unlighted
cigar, a nervous twitch pinching one side of his
face. He was dressed in tailor-made clothes of
good fabric but was undisturbed about the drying

mud caked on his shoes and his trouser cuffs. He was a slight, balding Yankee trader, a pleasant man to work for as long as you played it straight. Cheat him and you'd better never come back.

Posey shifted the cigar to the other side of his mouth. "Can't complain, the way some of the others have come in. Stump Johnson hardly had a wagonload."

"How about the hide prices?"

"A little better. Should get better yet. Prospect of a scarcity."

Jameson looked at the men sitting on the wagons, men bearded and dirty, with a trailweariness in their eyes.

"As long as prices are up, could you give the boys a little bonus? They haven't made much this trip."

Posey came about as near smiling as he ever would. "Maybe I can see my way clear." As the wagons pulled up and halted he spoke loudly, "You boys pile off of there and go over to the Dutchman's. Tell him I said give you a good feed. The yard crew can take care of the wagons."

The men jumped down laughing, exulting at the feel of Dodge's half-muddy ground beneath their feet.

"How about you, Gage?" Posey asked.

Jameson shrugged. "Not hungry. I'll go later."

Ever since he had arrived he had noticed a tall, well-dressed man of about his own age standing at the door of the shack, watching him, watching the wagons. Now Posey motioned to the man. "Come here, Ransom. Want you to meet somebody."

The man stepped forward, a smile lifting the

ends of his trimmed mustache. "You don't have to tell me. He's Gage Jameson. I've heard plenty already. My name's King, Jameson. Ransom King."

He stood an inch or two taller than Jameson. He wore black trousers and a white shirt with a string tie. His flat-brimmed hat with its rounded crown was as clean as a man could expect to find in a place like Dodge. Jameson wouldn't exactly call him a dandy, like Hickok or Cody, but he was well above the average cut. More than that, he looked like he might be man enough to wear the clothes and get away with it.

"Glad to know you, King. Seems to me I've heard the name around. Hide hunter, aren't you?"

King smiled. "That's right. Been hoping for a good while that we'd cross trails somewhere."

He turned then to Posey. "I can see you're going to be busy awhile, C.T., so I'll work on up the street and come back later. You sure you're not ready to meet my price on those hides?"

"Not yet," Posey answered with good humor. "You're just trying to make a killing on one deal so you can retire."

"Now, C.T.," King responded with a laugh, "that's not fair. You know I'm a man of simple tastes and a small ambition. All I want is to get rich."

He started to move away, a spark of laughter still dancing in his eyes. "See you later, C. T., and you'd just as well make up your mind to pay me my price. You're going to do it sooner or later anyway, so why not now?"

He reached for Jameson's hand again. "Glad

to've met you, Jameson. Perhaps we can get better acquainted over a bottle of good whisky, if you come down to Wash's saloon.''

"Maybe later,''Jameson said. As King walked away, Jameson looked to Posey with a question in his eyes. Posey answered it.

"Good hunter, that King. He's had luck right along, even with the buffalo playing out. And when it comes to selling, he's as independent as a hog on ice. I'll spar around with him a little, but in the end I'll have to give him what he's asking. I know it, and so does he."

Jameson tested the name on his tongue. "Ransom King. Sounds like something out of a book.''

Posey shrugged. "May be where he got it. Lots of people around here aren't using the names their mothers gave them.'' He turned and walked into his little frame office, Jameson following him. "That King,''Posey said, shaking his head. "They lost the pattern after they made him.''

He dug into a desk and brought out a record book. Blowing the dust off it, he asked, "Want to watch the yard crew count off the hides?''

"Won't be necessary.'' Jameson pulled a tally book out of his pocket. "Got the figures here for every wagon.''

Posey picked it up and riffled the pages. "And they'll be correct, too, right down to the last kip.'' Humor was in his eyes.

While Posey pulled open a door at the bottom of his heavy roll-top desk and brought out a bottle and two glasses, Jameson looked around the office. It was strictly a working man's setup, not meant for entertaining royalty. Papers were piled high and seemingly without care on top of the desk and the heavy iron safe in the corner. But Jameson would bet his Big Fifty, reloading outfit and all, that Posey knew where to find anything he needed. Not a single picture on the bare wall, but there was a solitary little calendar, notes scribbled in careful hand around many of the dates. Three Indian-tanned buffalo robes lay rolled up along one wall.

There was a faint aroma of tobacco and whisky, but it was overpowered by the strong smell of heavy grease and buffalo hides.

Once Jameson had asked Posey if the stink ever bothered him.

"Sometimes," came the bland comment, "when the prices start dropping."

Posey poured two shot glasses full. Jameson took his down in one long, appreciative swallow, his face squinching up at the burn of the whisky. It was good bourbon. Posey had it shipped to him all the way from Kentucky.

He eased out a long breath and nodded in approval. "First one I've had in months."

"Didn't you take some along for medicinal purposes?"

"We turned that wagon over the third week out. Broke every bottle but one. We *did* have to save that one for medicinal purposes."

He turned serious. "How does it look, C.T.?"

Posey shook his head. "Not good, Gage, not good. She's cutting mighty thin. You saw how many hunters are camped around town here. They've scoured the whole Arkansas. By spring there won't be enough hides left to sweat a pair of mules. Indians are restless, too. Cheyennes killed one of Stump Johnson's men.

"Trouble is, there's nowhere to go from here. The army's turning hunters back from the northern territory because of the Medicine Lodge treaty. And south—well, you know what's to the south."

Jameson squeezed the whisky glass. "The Cimarron. And below that, the Canadian. And buffalo, C.T. . . . there's bound to be a world of buffalo down there."

"And a world of Comanches."

Jameson looked directly into Posey's eyes. "Comanches or not, I want to go."

Posey straightened, taken aback. "Knowing you, I shouldn't be surprised. But I can't afford to send any Miles and Posey wagons down there. Not till I know we've got a better than even chance of bringing the men back alive and the wagons full of hides. Right now, I don't think we have that chance."

Jameson stood up and looked out the open door toward the hide wagons with their light load. "We haven't got much choice, have we? It's go south or pick bones. And C.T., I'm no bone picker."

Posey shrugged. "You're right, Gage. We both know it. But the question is, when? The time's not right, not yet."

"And when will the time be right? When somebody goes down there and proves it can be done. What's going to happen when somebody comes back from Texas with a string of wagons piled high with hides? I'll tell you. It won't matter if the whole outfit has arrows sticking out of it like the quills on a porcupine—men'll run all over each other trying to get down there. Price of wagons and teams will shoot up. You'll be offering two dollars a day—maybe three—trying to get skinners and teamsters.

"I want to be that first man."

Posey only stared at him. "I'd like to do it, Gage. I'd like to let you go. But Jason Miles is half of this partnership, and he'd hit the ceiling. Me, I'm the flighty type. I'll shoot the works on a scheme that looks halfway good. Jason is so hidebound he wouldn't invest a nickel if he couldn't see a dime lying in front of him. So we balance each other off. I keep Jason prodded along, and he keeps my feet on the ground. Right now, no amount of persuasion would move Jason Miles."

Jameson's eyes grew keen. He pointed his chin toward the big safe in the corner. "That money the company's been holding for me—got it at hand? Got it where I could get it if I wanted it right quick?"

Posey's face tightened in worry. "Yes, but what's going on in that Indian mind of yours?"

"Just this, C.T.: if Miles and Posey doesn't want to send me, I'll go on my own. There's buffalo down there in Texas. I'm going to get them!"

2

JAMESON STOOD at the door, watching the yard crew take up reins and holler at the heavy-muscled ox teams as they moved the hide wagons down to unload them at the end of the stacks. He noted that the crew was no longer so large as it used to be.

"The frontier's fading fast," he said. "So's the hide game. Man's got to make himself a stake now—get into something that'll last—or pretty soon there won't be much chance left. I'm thirty-five already. Forty's looking at me from around the corner. How many more years have I got to make myself a start, C.T.? I've got to do it soon or I'll be going around in circles like old Shad Blankenship.

"Shad doesn' know anything but the frontier. He can see it getting away from him, and he's scared. What's going to be left for him when it's gone? He's been out here since they dug the Arkansas River, and what's he got to show for it? What's he ever *going* to have? Nothing."

He squatted down in the doorway, in the manner of a man in camp, and leaned against the door-jamb. "I've saved money since I've been working for Miles and Posey, but it won't be enough. And I can't add much to it hanging around up here where the buffalo are all gone.

"So I'll take what money I've got and buy wagons with it, and supplies. I'll hire me a tough crew and go down where the buffalo are. Sure, I know it's risky. But what that ever amounted to anything wasn't a gamble?"

Posey studied him long and hard. He leaned down and filled Jameson's glass again, then his own.

"You're right, Gage. You generally are. But what kind of outfit could you put together with the money you've got, and still buy supplies? Five or six wagons at the outside. How many men could you hire, even if you found some willing to go? Not enough to put up much defense. The Comanches could swallow up a little outfit in five minutes. You need a big one."

Posey had a way of looking at a man and into him.

"There's more to it than just the money, Gage. What else is it?"

Fingering the glass, staring out at the sweating yard crew, Jameson was a minute in answering.

"You didn't see this country before the hide hunters got thick, C. T. But I did. I came out here with a freighting outfit when I was just a kid. There was nothing but a few army posts along the immigrant trails. Stray off a few miles and you were in land only a handful of white men had ever seen. Every kind of wild game you could imagine. And the plains themselves, reaching on and on as far as a man could see, just the way it must have been when God finished it.

"It wasn't all littered up with buffalo bones, or houses, or railroads, or busted-down wagons. It wasn't spotted with rotting corpses.

"And the buffalo . . . I've seen them in herds so big that in the rutting season you could hear the bulls fighting from miles away. I've seen a big herd on winter mornings with the steam hanging low over them like a cloud of smoke. Once a man sees those things, they're never really out of his mind again. He never forgets. He doesn't know what they mean to him till they're gone. Then he keeps looking, hoping maybe he'll find it somewhere else.

"Maybe that's a big part of it, C. T. Maybe down there I'll find it again the way it used to be. And even if I don't, I won't be satisfied till I've gone and looked."

Posey had chewed his cigar down to half size. "And what if you *do* find it? It'll be spoiled again in a little while. You'll help spoil it yourself."

Jameson said ruefully, "Funny, isn't it? We thought it would stay like that forever. Seemed like the country was so big that nothing we did would matter. But we spoiled it. Now I'm ready to go along and watch it happen all over, just to get to see it once again the way it used to be."

Posey sat awhile, frowning, that nervous twitch in his face as he studied his hands and chewed his cigar. He was deep in thought. Finally he spoke. "Look, Gage, I've got money of my own, money Jason Miles hasn't got any claim on. You go on and

22

buy whatever you need. Make it big enough so you can defend yourself. I'll back you just as far as you need to go.''

Jameson stood there like someone had clubbed him.

''C. T., I . . . I don't hardly know what to say.''

''You don't have to say anything. Just come back.''

Jameson rubbed his smooth-shaven chin and looked at himself in the barber's cracked mirror. He had to grin at the whiteness of his face where whiskers had shielded his skin from sun and wind since he had taken the wagons out months ago. On the rough floor at his feet lay a thick mat of hair that the barber had whacked off. The short hair felt unnatural now, freshly washed out with strong soap.

The barber said, ''Better watch yourself a day or two till you get used to it, or you'll catch cold. You're like a fresh-sheared sheep.''

Behind a partition stood a big wooden washtub, more than half full of cold water. Two buckets bubbled and steamed atop a big cast-iron heater. The barber slowly poured their contents into the tub, then stirred until the water was evenly warm.

Over the back of a wooden chair Jameson draped a suit of clean new clothes he had bought down the street. Undressing, he threw the dirty clothes into a corner, far from the clean ones. He settled into the warm water for a long, comfortable soak, lighting a black cigar and leaning back relaxed, wondering if a man could ever get all the buffalo smell off.

A barber sees about as many people as anybody in town except maybe a bartender. Jameson called to him beyond the partition.

"Heard anybody quote prices on wagons and teams lately?"

The barber was sweeping the hair into a dusty pile to throw it out the back door. "If you got any to sell, you're hubbin' it, mister. There's plenty for sale and mighty few buyers."

"I was thinking I might buy a few wagons and a good string of mules if the price was right."

The barber stopped sweeping and looked around the partition. "Better not say that too loud. They'll run over you."

Jameson picked up the rough brown bar of soap and began to rub it briskly over his wet arms and shoulders. "You might spread the word that I'm in the market. Name's Gage Jameson. With Miles and Posey."

Bath finished, he strode far down to the edge of town, where an aging Negro woman lived in a rude shack close to the riverbank. She did washing and ironing while her husband helped hustle teams at the Miles and Posey yards. Under his arm Jameson carried a sackful of dirty clothes, on his shoulder his bedroll.

He found Callie out back of the shack, shoving firewood into the flames under a huge smoke-blackened pot full of boiling water, a big red neckerchief tied over her hair.

Seeing him, she dropped the wood and began to shake excitedly, grinning broadly as if he had come back from the dead. "Mister Gage, Mister

Gage. I declare I thought them Injuns had got you."

"Callie, I was so dirty they were afraid to touch me."

He dropped the sack on the ground, along with the bedroll. "Brought some clothes and some bedding. Wish you'd give every bit of it a good slow boiling, right down to the last pair of socks."

She shook her head. "I'll do it, but boilin' is almighty hard on clothes. These buffalo hunters do beat all, the way they want their stuff boiled."

He grinned. "Callie, I've seen men bet a hundred dollars on which one could reach in his pocket and come up with a louse first. That's why we boil our clothes."

He looked at the poor frame shack she lived in, and pity moved him. Once he had asked the old woman about it, and she had told him of the good cabin she and Rufe had shared in Georgia, before freedom. Then she had added with a fierce pride, "I wouldn't trade back, Mister Gage. This one, it ain't much. But it's all ours."

He dug into his new coat and brought up a paper-wrapped package. "Got something here for you. Traded it off of old Limping Wolf's Sioux when we came across them a while back."

Excitedly she tore the paper off and found a pair of fancy leather moccasins with a fine job of beadwork. Her eyes widened, and her white teeth gleamed proudly. The she sobered.

"Mister Gage, you shouldn't of. With all the pretty girls there is in town, you could've found you a good one to give them to."

Gage said evenly, "There are pretty ones, but there aren't many good ones. That's why I got the moccasins for you."

Later he walked through the open door of a frame dance hall, pausing to let his eyes accustom themselves to the dimmer light indoors. A chubby barman gave him a crooked-toothed grin and lifted a big hand in greeting.

"Jameson. Gage Jameson!" He held a bottle high, beckoning with his chin. "It's on me, Gage."

Shaking hands, Jameson looked out over the room. Not much business yet. Some of his own crew sat at a big table, drinking and playing cards. They nodded at him.

"How's business, Wash?" Jameson asked while the man poured each of them a drink.

Wash had been a buffalo hunter too, but he had early decided there must be some easier way to make a living. And he hadn't been able to think of anything with so steady and sure a trade as the whisky business. Once he had tried to talk Jameson into going in partnership with him. But Jameson hadn't been able to picture himself as a saloon keeper. Sure, he was looking for something that would beat buffalo hunting. But this wasn't it.

"Business is getting slow, Gage," Wash complained. "Hide trade is falling off fast. Should've set up in Wichita or Ellsworth, I reckon. Cattle drives from Texas really pour the silver into those towns. They tell me a cowboy ain't got no bottom to him when it comes to putting away drinking liquor. But I don't suppose Dodge City will ever get any of that cattle trade. We come too late."

Jameson finished his friendly drink with Wash, then angled across the room to where the lanky skinner Messick sat at a corner table, laboriously scrawling a letter. Jameson pulled out a chair and sat down facing him.

Painfully Messick said, "Writin' to my sister. Got to tell her about George Hobart."

Jameson nodded. "That's what I figured."

The memory of it brought an angry twist to his face—the sight of three men lying dead in the remains of a hide camp, wagons and stock gone, their bodies ripped by gunfire, slashed by knives.

"How much are you going to tell her?"

"Just that her husband is dead, and we found him there. What else can I say? I can't tell her what they did to him—the way they scalped him and . . ."

Messick broke off, long face purpling.

"Worst job of butchery I ever saw," Jameson said. "No old warrior would've taken any pride in it. Young bucks, maybe. Likely got ahold of some firewater."

Messick's eyes narrowed with rekindled anger. "And maybe it wasn't Indians at all. Maybe it was hide thieves, coverin' up. Wagons was gone, you know."

Jameson shrugged. Messick had spent a lot of time among Indians, and he liked them. "It was probably Indians, all right. They're stirred up over the buffalo killing. But we'll never know."

He stood up again, digging into his pocket. He brought out forty dollars and looked at it a moment. He'd spend it here anyway. Might as well see it go where it was needed.

He pitched the money onto the table. "Put this in with the letter. Tell her we found it in his pocket."

Jameson started to walk back to where the rest of the Miles and Posey crew sat. Just then a man shoved through the door, slammed it shut behind him and hollered in high good humor. "Whisky for everybody, Wash!"

It was Ransom King. He stood there chewing on a black cigar that must have been a foot long. His teeth gleamed happily beneath his trimmed mustache. "Sold my hides," he announced loudly for everyone to hear. "Got my own price, and it was a honey. Go on up, boys, don't be bashful. And don't let Wash give you the cheap stuff."

King moved to the bar, leaned over it, and reached way down, bringing up a bottle. He had known just where it would be. He looked at it quizzically, seeing that half of it was gone.

"Hey, Jameson," he called, "come on over and have one with me. Told you I'd get my price out of Posey."

Jameson grinned. It had been a long time since he'd met anyone like Ransom King. King caught his elbow and gave him a gentle shove toward a chair. "Sit down, my friend, and let's drink a toast to salesmanship."

Seated, Jameson noted that the bottle in King's hand held good whisky, if the label didn't lie. It wasn't the stuff Wash commonly served over the bar. It struck Jameson that King was the kind who would know what was the best and make sure he got it.

King poured them each a drink and lifted his glass. "Here's to the buffalo."

Jameson downed his with care, for another free drink or two would leave him walking on air, unused to it as he was. King took his with one swallow, cleared his throat and poured a second one. Jameson put his hand over his own glass, declining another.

King walked to a set of wooden stairs that started in a back corner and disappeared into the high ceiling.

"Hey, Rose," he shouted, "come on down here."

He came back without yelling again. Jameson smiled. "Sure she heard you?"

"She heard me," King replied confidently. "She listens for me."

He scratched a match across the seat of his good pants and held the flame to the end of the twisted cigar until the tobacco began to glow. He puffed big clouds of strong smoke, getting the cigar going, squinting his eyes against the smoke's bite.

"Yes sir," he said, "with those hide stacks dwindling down, old C. T. isn't in any position to haggle over a good bag of hides. He's got to pay for them. You ought to have heard him holler."

The thought of it struck King funny. He threw his head back and laughed. At first Jameson thought he might have emptied a bottle or two before he had ever come in here. Then he decided this was just the way King acted when he was feeling good.

He wondered how King might act if he felt bad. Even with the laughter there was a steel-keen look to King's square face. No doubt those sparkling eyes could as easily turn to flint.

A woman came down the stairs, trying to be graceful but lacking the ability. Dark-haired, young, she wore a golden gown cut low in front with two thin straps up over her wide, soft shoulders. The dress fit tightly against her ample upper body and down over her trim hips.

"See there?" King winked. "Told you she heard me."

He pushed to his feet and strode across to take her by the arm. "Come on over, Rose, and meet a real buffalo hunter. Rose Tremaine, this is Gage Jameson. They say he's even better than me."

Rose smiled at Jameson. He nodded and spoke to her. He remembered having seen her here before. And not with King.

"Sold those hides, sweetie," King said, pinching her chin so hard that it was white a moment, then red. "We'll celebrate a little tonight, you and me."

King walked over to the scuffed piano. The cigar sticking up at a jaunty angle, he picked out a rowdy dance hall tune with one finger. "Give us a little music, Rose," he said.

By this time everybody was watching Rose, and Jameson could see in her brown eyes how she glorified in this admiration. She seated herself at the piano and began to play and sing the tune King had started. King stood awhile with his elbow on the piano, watching her like a hungry cat watching a mouse. Finally he walked back to the table where Jameson sat.

"Quite a gal, that one," King said.

Jameson nodded. She did look mighty good to a man who had been three months out on the buffalo range.

"You ought to get acquainted with her, Jameson," King said.

"Looks to me like you've already got the deed."

King shrugged. "Women are all right for a while, for a little diversion. Can't seem to get along without them. But you get tired of one after so long. I've been hoping someone would come along and take Rose off my hands. Man needs a change in diet occasionally."

Jameson smiled, thinking he might be tempted if he didn't have so much of more importance on his mind.

King poured himself a third drink. As quickly as it had come, the laughter went out of his face and he turned serious.

"Barber told me you're in the market for wagons and teams."

"That's right."

"I've done some thinking about it. The way I see it, you must be planning to go south."

Jameson looked at him in surprise. King explained, "You're a man of considerable reputation as a hunter, Jameson. You wouldn't waste money on wagons to hunt in this country. The army's not letting anybody up into that northern territory. So you *must* be going south."

Jameson studied King's changeable face, wondering what the man was aiming at.

"There's buffalo down there, Jameson," King said with enthusiasm. "Big herds that can load a man's wagons with flint hides in a hurry. I've seen a few of them, just enough to set my blood to racing and the seat of my pants to itching. I took four wagons south of the Arkansas last spring. But you could fairly smell Indian in the air. Half my men panicked and deserted me. I had to turn back before we had skinned out a wagonload.

"A man could make himself a small fortune down there, Jameson, a first-rate hunter with plenty of guts and more than common judgment. They tell me you're that kind of man."

Jameson took the compliment without reply, knowing King was working up to something.

"Main thing," King said, "would be to take enough men and wagons that an outfit could defend itself. The Comanches aren't foolish. They fight when they think they can win. When they don't think they can, they don't try."

He drank half the whisky out of his glass and pointed his finger at Jameson. "Now it happens I know a man who has a string of wagons and all the teams you'll need. He'll sell them cheap. Tell you what, you make the rounds and price the wagons and mules that you find. Whatever kind of deal you're offered, my man'll do better, I guarantee you."

Jameson eyed him levelly. "Where's your profit, King? You're not doing this for nothing."

King broke into a high, loud laugh. "They were right about you, Jameson, you're a perceptive man. All right, I have a motive of my own. I wanted to get on your warm side so you'd let me take my own wagons with you into Texas. I wasn't going to make that proposition until I'd built you

32

up for it. But there it is.''

Jameson rubbed his chin thoughtfully, then slowly shook his head. "This is going to be my own expedition, King. I don't want to have to consult anybody or worry what anybody else thinks. I'm my own boss. You can't be that way when there's another outfit with you. I've seen too many hunters go off together, then fall out. No real leader, everybody a free agent. A little friction starts and you're done for."

"There won't be any conflict. You'll be the wagon master. What you say goes, any time."

Jameson shook his head. "I'm sorry, King."

Ransom King studied Jameson, his eyes unreadable. Presently he shrugged. "No harm done, and no hard feelings. What I said about those wagons still stands. Come around to my camp when you've priced the others. My man'll make you a better deal."

Jameson smiled a little. "No motive this time?"

King laughed. "He owes me money, and I want to get paid." He looked at Rose, and he looked at the stairs. "See you tomorrow, Jameson?"

Jameson nodded, beginning to like this tall, brash man. "Tomorrow."

Old Shad Blankenship was pacing impatiently about his camp when Jameson rode up into the firelight.

"About decided you wasn't comin' after all," he said half peevishly, raking the fire restlessly with a stick. "Been dark an hour. Thought you'd found you some redheaded filly and plumb forgot about that bottle you were going to bring me."

"Now, Shad," Jameson grinned, "do you think a filly could make me forget the man who taught me how to shoot a buffalo gun and talk sign language and cure out a green hide?"

A flicker of humor showed behind Shad's deep scowl as he grabbed the bottle from Jameson's hand and began to worry the cork out of it.

"If she couldn't, you're a sight older than I think you are. When I was a few years younger a filly could make me forget my own name. Way it is, the whisky's all that's left for me. That and the cards."

There wasn't a great deal of the whisky left, either, by the time Shad finally laid the bottle aside, wiping his hand on his ancient, deep-stained old buckskin jacket from which most of the fringe was long since gone. Shad frowned at Jameson as the glow began to work upward in him.

"Now what's this foolishness I hear about you wantin' to buy wagons and mules?"

"Where did you hear it?"

"Man, it spread over town like the cholera through an Injun camp. Been a dozen men here to ask me about you. Have you plumb lost your head?"

"I hope not."

"What good is wagons when the buffalo is gone?"

"There's buffalo to the south, Shad."

Blankenship snorted and uncorked the bottle again. "Jason Miles would jump ten feet and fall over dead."

"He's not in on it. Just C. T. Posey and me."

Shad stared hard at Jameson until he was sure the younger man wasn't joshing him. "Then you *have* lost your head.''

"Shad, sooner or later somebody's going to go down there. It had just as well be me.''

Blankenship narrowed his eyes, and he slowly shook his head. "Come spring, your scalp'll be dried and hanging from some heathen Comanche's lodgepole, that's for sure. But don't listen to me. Go on down there and get yourself knocked over.''

He held the bottle out to arm's length, trying to read the label. ''Just let me get my paws on some of your money first. You want to buy wagons? All right, I'll sell you mine.''

Jameson looked sharply at him. "Sell me yours? What would you ever do, Shad? You've been a hide man so long you'd starve to death trying to make an honest living.'

"The hide business is goin' to the devil, and I ain't makin' the trip with it. I'm heading back to the settlements and take up farming, like I told you.''

"It wouldn't last a month. You'd be back out here skinning buffalo if you had to walk the whole way barefooted.''

Shad Blankenship flared, the whisky beginning to get him. "A man crazy enough to do what you're figuring on ain't in no shape to be givin' advice. Just buy my wagons. Three of them, and the teams—the whole works, tools, camp gear, lock, stock and barrel—for a thousand dollars. And cheap at the price.''

Studying the old man, Jameson wished Shad hadn't said it. The outfit was worth far more than he was asking for it.

"Shad, that's the whisky talking. Let's let it wait till morning.''

"If you don't buy it, I'll sell it to somebody else."

Jameson finally shrugged. "All right, if that's the way it's got to be, you've just sold out. What say I give you a hundred of it here and send the rest on ahead?"

Blankenship shook his head, angering. The hint was plain enough—he couldn't take care of the money.

"I'll take it all right now, right here, thankee."

"Shad, you won't get out of town with a dime of it."

Blankenship arose quickly, his fists knotting. "By Judas Priest, you listen to me, young'un! I was a grown man trapping beaver and dodging the Blackfeet before your Maw and Paw ever even thought of you. Don't you think I got sense enough to know what I'm about? You just pay me, that's all you got to do."

Unwillingly Jameson said, "All right, Shad, however you want it."

He knew what would happen as soon as Shad got his hands on the cash. He had seen it too many times.

"Look, Shad, keep your wagons. Come with me to Texas. We'll split the take according to what each man puts in."

It was exactly the deal he had turned down for Ransom King. But he knew Shad Blankenship. Shad would be worth three of most men, if he ever got out of Dodge.

But Shad's feelings were hurt. "I ain't gonna take orders from you, young'un, just because you got the most wagons. No, sir, you just take me to town and pay me off, right now. I'm goin' to Missouri."

Jameson spent most of the next day riding through the camps scattered up and down the river, looking at wagons and mules. He found many men eager to sell. The prices they quoted him were low compared to what they had been last spring.

He could have gotten oxen even cheaper, but winter was coming on. Mules would be better for the long haul where feed had to be carried. And mules were faster in a pinch. Trouble with mules, the Indians liked them too. Nothing appealed to an Indian's horse-stealing tendencies more than the thought of a fat mule's hind leg smoking over an open fire.

Late in the day, before angling toward Ransom King's camp, Jameson stopped to see Shad Blankenship. One look at Shad's pain-twisted face, his sick and stricken eyes, told him the whole story.

"I been a first-class fool, Gage," the old man lamented, running his gnarled fingers miserably through his rusty mat of long hair. "You had me pegged right enough. I got drunk and fell into a poker game. Them highbinders melted my roll like a snowbank in August. I ain't goin' to Missouri. I ain't even got the cash to get out of Dodge."

There was no use saying I told you so, even if Jameson had been of a mind to. He laid a hand on Shad's shoulder and sat down beside him on the dirty old buffalo robe the hunter had spread out inside his grimy tent. He looked at Shad with sorrow in his eyes, and a disturbing thought took hold of him:

A few more years the way I'm going and I'll be just like him.

That was why he *had* to go down and find that Texas herd, had to make him a stake now while there was still time.

"How about going south with me, Shad?"

"I'd be in your way. I ain't got sense enough to get in out of the rain."

"Shad, you're still the best hide man in the business, barring none. I'll be needing your advice down there."

"You're just feeling sorry for me. You got no call to."

"That's not it. I need those sharp eyes of yours. There's few hunters can bring down as many buffalo as you can and smoke up as few cartridges doing it. You didn't lose your rifle in that poker game, did you?"

"No."

"Then oil it up. You'll be using it."

3

RANSOM KING shifted to one side in the saddle. "Yonder's his camp," he said. "Looks like a hog sty, but he's got the goods to sell."

The wagons were scattered around in no particular order, some of the harness done up on the wheels, some of it thrown carelessly out on the ground. Cooking utensils lay about, unwashed, some of them caked up with dried-out food. The whole place had an unpleasant odor to it that wrinkled Jameson's nose.

Jameson counted the wagons to himself, raising and dropping his hand. Six doubles and a single. They were of several kinds and of various sizes, as if they had been picked up a few at a time. Most were good Studebaker wagons or their equals. A few wouldn't do for a bone hauler.

A bulky man walked out slowly, carrying himself with a deliberate ease that tried to say he wasn't afraid of anybody in the world.

But Jameson's keen eye told him this bearded

man was only a weak imitation, a bluff, hollow inside.

"Gage Jameson, Adam Budge," King said by way of introduction.

Budge shook hands but stared belligerently with black eyes, as if this transaction wasn't going to be to his liking. His hands were grimy, his black beard dirty and greasy. Half the buttons were gone from his salt-crusted shirt.

The man stood awkwardly a minute before he broke his silence. "King says you want to buy wagons. I got them to sell."

Jameson nodded. "Tell you right now, I've had some cheap prices quoted to me today."

Budge glanced questioningly at King. King said, "Whatever they are, Budge'll beat them. You want to look over the outfit?"

Jameson walked among the wagons, carefully checking under them and over them. Finally he said, "Three would have to come out. I'll take the others, if the price is right. Now how about the mules?"

"Down on the riverbank," Budge said. "Got a man herding them."

An unkempt stock tender sat on the ground, holding an old horse that stood hip-shot. He had the mules bunched loosely on the grass not far from water.

Jameson rode slowly into them, looking for harness sores, making the mules move around so he could tell if any of them limped. He found a cripple or two that way and eased them out of the bunch. He cut back a couple of old and unthrifty mules that might have a hard time getting through the

winter, and on a long haul at that. He looked for
well-built animals with long legs placed solidly
under their bodies like the legs under a table. He
looked for flat backs, good head, good ear, good
foot and bone. He cut back two or three narrow-
bodied mules with legs too close together that
indicated a lack of stamina. He always remembered what Shad had told him once about picking
mules.

"You see one that's got forelegs comin' out of
the same hole like a rabbit's, you leave him alone.
One knee says to the other, 'You let me by this time
and I'll let you by the next.' "

A wild-eyed mule wheeled as Jameson came to
him. He lashed out with a hind foot and narrowly
missed Jameson's leg. Quickly Jameson cut him
out, too. He didn't want any fractious mule getting
a whole team in a jackpot and tearing up a pair of
wagons, especially wagons loaded with flint hides
that might fetch two dollars or more apiece.

Back in camp, Ransom King sought out cups
from a wooden box in a wagon bed and poured
coffee. Jameson looked dubiously at his cup,
which had a thin scum of grease on it. His eyes
caught King's and he knew King had the same
thought. But Jameson had been around hide
camps so much that it took a lot to make him sick.
For courtesy's sake he sipped the bitter black coffee without comment.

Budge scowled over his own coffee. "All
right," he said sharply, "what'll you give?"

Jameson leaned forward setting the cup down.
"Well, I've had good wagons offered to me as
cheap as three hundred dollars a pair, and mules at

fifty a head. I know that's a mighty little, but some of these boys are desperate."

Jameson felt a pleasant tremor of excitement, the tingle that always came to him when he was trying to make a close trade. He was that much like Posey. This was cheaper than he had ever hoped for. Used to be that a good new wagon and a well-matched team could run a man an easy thousand dollars.

Budge chewed his whiskered lip, showing a set of yellow teeth streaked brown from tobacco. "Last spring they was worth a sight more."

Jameson shrugged, keeping his face bland. "I can buy them from somebody else."

King said, "Budge will sell them to you."

Budge nodded his shaggy head, the reluctant words dragging from him like pulled teeth. "Yeah, yeah, I reckon so."

Jameson said, "Four thousand even for the ten wagons and that string of mules, minus the ones I cut out. All right?"

Budge sloshed his coffee around, trying to get the sugar up off the bottom of the cup. He drank, then wiped a filthy sleeve across his mouth. "Yeah, I reckon that'll have to do."

Jameson relaxed slowly, letting out a long breath. For weeks on the prairie he'd thought about taking his own expedition south if Miles and Posey didn't go for the idea. He hadn't let himself hope for anywhere near this many wagons.

"When do you want to be paid?" Jameson asked.

Budge said, "I want to square up a few accounts"—he flicked a half-resentful glance at

King—"and catch the first train East. I'd be obliged if you paid me tonight."

"How about coming to the Miles and Posey office with me?"

Budge shook his head. "Can't. I got to go see a man who'll take them cut back mules and extra wagons off my hands. He'll rob me, but leastways I can get the money tonight and catch that train."

He scratched his black chin. "You know where the Queen of the Arkansas Saloon is?"

Jameson nodded. It was a rat hole of a place, a half dugout on the wrong side of the tracks. Cheap whisky, low-stakes poker.

Budge said, "The man I got to see owns the place. Why don't you meet me there?"

Jameson wasn't sure it suited him, carrying four thousand dollars in cash. It would be well dark before he got back. But he had seen hide buyers moving around freely all over Dodge in the past, their pockets stuffed with greenbacks. If anybody ever molested them, he hadn't heard about it.

"All right," he said, dismissing the thought. He looked at King. "Ready to go?"

Riding away, King smiled. "You got you a great buy back there."

"I know it. Just one thing worries me. Budge isn't the type. A skinner or a teamster, maybe, but not a man to own and boss a string of wagons."

King shrugged. "Maybe he's found that out. That's why he's selling."

"What kind of a squeeze have you got on him, King?"

"I just told him I was tired of waiting, and if he didn't pay me I'd peel the hide off of him, an inch at a time. He looks rough, Jameson, but he's as scary as a squawking old hen.''

Jameson caught C. T. Posey just as he was closing his office, and got the four thousand dollars in cash out of the big safe. He shoved it into the deep pocket of his coat. Then he strapped his six-shooter on over the coat, just in case.

It wasn't far to the saloon, so he unsaddled his horse and turned him loose in the company yard. Then he walked over the tracks and down on the other side.

None of Dodge City looked very polished or respectable, but here was the seamiest part of it, raw frame saloons and dance halls, others built of nothing more than sod, a few even dug into the ground, only the top half reaching above ground level. He heard fiddle music and rough laughter. Yonder he saw a woman standing watching him, the yellow flicker of lamplight behind her outlining her in a doorway. She spoke to him, but he didn't catch the words and didn't want to.

A lantern hung on either side of the door at the Queen of the Arkansas, yellow flame licking at the wick. The nearly flat sod roof was only waist-high to Jameson, most of the building being dug into the ground. He thought idly what would happen to this place if a sudden cloudburst should send water cascading down the street. It would fill up like a jug.

A match suddenly flared, and a man's face glowed as he touched the flame to a cigarette. ''You Jameson?''

''Yes.''

''Then go on inside. Budge is waitin' for you.''

Vaguely disturbed, Jameson hesitated a moment, looking through the ground-level windows and seeing light inside. Carefully then, he moved down the warped wooden steps to the sunken doorway.

The wall-trapped reek of smoke and whisky and unwashed bodies slapped him in the face. It reminded him of a wolf den he had crawled into once. This was like it, more den than house.

The light was dim, for the owner was stingy with his lanterns. But Jameson easily spotted Adam Budge's bulk. He sat at a table with another man, his broad back turned to the door. His shirt was soaked with sweat. The man at the table looked up at Jameson. He was a cheap gambler, Jameson remembered, who went by the name of Frenchy. Dirty, unkempt, he was not in the class with the gamblers who stayed around the bigger places.

Budge licked his lips, and his voice had a high pitch to it. "Jameson, c-c-come on over."

Jameson hesitated, with a sudden quickening of alarm. Budge is scared half to death, he thought. His hand moved down toward the six-shooter.

"Hold it, friend!" The words were short-clipped. Jameson glanced quickly at the bar. The tender held a shotgun, aimed straight at him.

"Go shut the door, Mick," said Frenchy. The man behind Jameson shoved the door shut and took the bartender's shotgun. "Now come on over," Frenchy said to Jameson. Jameson slowly stepped forward, looking into the muzzle of Frenchy's derringer, knowing the shotgun was at his back. He felt his six-shooter being jerked from the holster.

Budge's chin was trembling. So were his hands, placed judiciously on the table where all could see them.

"Now," said Frenchy, rising to his feet, "where is it?"

"Where is what?" Jameson bluffed, knowing it was a waste of time.

"The money. You got it. Budge has told us all about it."

Budge's voice shrilled desperately, "Jameson, they're fixin' to kill us!"

Jameson said, "Somebody's steered you wrong. There isn't any money."

In the back of his mind was a wild hope that when they reached for him to search him, he might grab a gun.

So suddenly he didn't see it, a leather whip or something lashed at his face. A cry swelled in his throat, and he bent over, his hands clawing at the fire which seared his cheeks.

"Don't stall me around," Frenchy gritted. "Where's that money?"

Jameson made no reply, clenching his teeth against the burn. The lash struck again, across the back of his neck.

"Search him."

Rough hands jerked him around. Through pain-reddened eyes Jameson saw that the man behind him had set the shotgun down, just out of his reach. Hands dug into his coat pockets.

"Here it is, Frenchy. Holy smoke, look at them greenbacks!"

For a second then, while they feverishly eyed the money, Jameson thought he might have a chance. He reached for the shotgun. But someone was ready. A gun barrel slanted across his skull, sent him sprawling on the packed dirt floor amid cigarette butts and dried tobacco juice. He lay half conscious, brain hammering with pain.

"Supposed to be four thousand there," someone said. "Count it."

They ran through it and satisfied themselves.

The bartender said, "What're we gonna do with them two? Can't have them runnin' loose. Give me the word, Frenchy, and I'll shoot them both."

"No," replied Frenchy, more concerned over the money than over the men. "Too much noise. Knife's just as good and a heap quieter."

A cry of terror from Adam Budge helped bring Jameson groping back to consciousness. "Don't do it," Budge quaked. "I won't tell nobody, Frenchy, I swear it. You can keep the money, only don't do it."

Budge arose shaking, letting his chair fall back across Jameson's legs. He began to dodge away from the man with the knife. He kept crying, "No, Frenchy, no!" He pushed the table out, trying to keep it between them.

Without moving, Jameson sought the shotgun with his eyes. It still stood where it had been, propped against the sod wall. A slim chance, but the only one he had.

The door burst open. Two men stood there, guns in their hands. In the split second before the guns roared, Jameson recognized Ransom King and saw a wild fever in the man's eyes that was like a look into hell. Jameson grabbed for the shotgun, got it, and rolled over onto his back.

He saw the bartender drop the knife and spin away from the force of the first two bullets, then fall, limp as a sack of grain. Frenchy whirled toward the door, bringing up the derringer. Jameson swung the shotgun around and squeezed the trigger, the roar of it swelling like a dynamite blast in the tiny room. The impact slammed Frenchy against the wall. He fell forward then and lay crumpled, his fingers convulsively digging into the packed earth.

The third man cowered back, raising his hands.

Beside King stood a heavy-bodied man with ragged beard, wolf-gray eyes shining in savage pleasure. He turned his six-gun to the third man and shot him where he stood, triggering two more bullets into his body after he fell.

"That's enough, Trencher." King spoke sharply.

"I reckon it is," the man called Trencher replied calmly. "He's dead." His eyes glittered, his wide mouth lifting a little at the corners. Standing there in the heavy, circling cloud of gun smoke, he flexed his gun hand nervously, eyes flicking back and forth among the fallen men, as if hoping one of them might move a little.

But they never would again.

Jameson pushed up weakly, leaning against the dirt wall and rubbing the back of his head where the gun barrel had struck him.

Budge was on his knees along the same wall, his face chalk-white, his body shaking so Jameson could actually hear his teeth clicking. Budge tried to talk, but all that would come from his throat was a hollow squeak.

Ransom King stepped behind the bar and picked up a bottle. He blew dust from a glass and poured it half full. He handed it across to Jameson. "Here. You need this."

Jameson downed most of it and braced himself against its fiery jolt.

King lifted the bottle to his lips and took a long pull. Face suddenly flushed and twisted, he spat it out across the bar. "Wow!" he exclaimed. "Man who'd sell stuff like that doesn't deserve to live anyhow."

He walked out from behind the bar and handed the bottle to the trembling Budge.

"Buck up, Budge, and drink this. We got some money to count."

The whole thing had happened in the span of a few seconds. Now that it was over, reaction set in. Jameson's hands began to quiver, a little like Budge's. He pulled up a chair and sat down to let the spell pass, drinking a little more of the poor whisky in an effort to settle himself. He grinned sheepishly. "Some time to get scared, now that it's over."

King shrugged. "Man who doesn't get scared once in a while is the rankest kind of a fool."

"You were just in time," Jameson said. "How did you know?"

King grinned then, the tension gone. "I didn't. It was just luck. Budge there isn't exactly a paragon of virtue. I got to thinking how easy it would be for him to take the money, quick as you paid him, and skip out on our little debt. The more I thought about it, the more worried I got. So I came over here to keep him honest. Just happened to peep in that window yonder first, and saw what the deal was."

Jameson sat there, letting the strength come back to him as he watched the big man Trencher filling his deep coat pockets with bottles from behind the bar.

Finally he said, "King, after this, if there's ever anything you want, just let me know."

King smiled. "Well now, as a matter of fact, there is. I still want to take my wagons to Texas with you."

Jameson looked down at the dead men sprawled out on the dirt floor.

"After this, how could I say no?"

4

SHARP COLD clung to the early-morning air. Gage Jameson looked at the stars and shivered. He fastened the top button of his woolen coat, wondering why it always took so long to shake the chill when a man was fresh out of bed.

He ate breakfast at the Dutchman's. He had arranged for the Dutchman to feed his men so they could get started without the delay that came from cooking and washing all the camp utensils. Besides, it was likely to be the last town meal they would get for a long time.

"My bunch all been in?" he asked, sipping his hot coffee and chewing on a thick slice of sugar-cured buffalo ham.

The stout old cook shrugged. "*Ach,* and more. You say please to feed fifteen men. It is already more than thirty that have come. I think you got a bunch of bums say they with you and they not."

Jameson frowned, until the humor of it touched him. He ought to have known the word would get around. Finishing up, he gave the old man twenty dollars.

"That cover it?"

The cook nodded vigorously, rubbing his stubby fingers over the paper money as if it had been silk. "*Ja, ja,* and you come again soon *wieder*."

Soberly Jameson said, "I hope so."

He walked briskly on down to the yards, the coffee and the hot meal making him warmer now. He could hear the restless stir of men and mules, the rattle of trace chains and the popping of leather as teams were pulled into place and hitched to the wagons. Men laughed and cursed and hollered one to another. Mules balked. Mules squealed and kicked. He heard the quick gust of breath from one as another's hind feet slammed into its stomach. A man yelled, and leather slapped hard across a mule's rump.

Jameson caught his horse and threw his heavy saddle across its back. He rubbed his hand over the saddle, liking the feel of it. It was one he had just bought, one somebody had picked up from a Texas trail hand in a cow town down the tracks. High cantle, high horn to tie a rope to. It was sturdily built, and Jameson thought it would be like riding a rocking chair after the light saddles he had been used to.

He looked up into the sky and picked out the Dipper, then the North Star. It wasn't easy to find now, for daylight was rapidly washing it out. He turned his back on the star and looked ahead in the direction to which the wagon tongues were pointed.

South. South across the deadline. South toward Texas.

Nervousness began to ripple in him now that the time was upon him. It always did when he set off for someplace he'd never been. He began itching to be on the move.

He would be glad to get away from Dodge again, away from its evil-smelling saloons, its gambling dens, the shady men who hung around them—not hunters, not men who toiled with leather-tough hands, but leeches who stole from other men what they had earned with their sweat, and sometimes with their blood.

Yet he could remember the eagerness with which he had gone into Dodge, an eagerness that seemed to grow a little more each trip. A taste for the whisky, a desire to play a little poker, an urge to look at the girls.

It wasn't what he really wanted, yet it was here, unbidden, and it was growing, a general aimlessness that eventually would put him in the same shape as old Shad Blankenship. There was no hope for Shad. He was too old to change.

Jameson wondered if soon there might no longer be hope for himself. Dodge was a reminder to him that time was going on, that he didn't have long left to find something permanent, something he could anchor to and hold solid.

He swung into the saddle and walked his bay horse down the line of wagons, seeing that the mules were harnessed up. He checked the trail

wagons in each pair, making sure their short
tongues were firmly bolted to the coupling poles of
the lead wagons. His horse stepped gingerly, the
bite of nippy air bringing out a touch of bronc that
still slept within him.

Up at the head of the line he came to the chuck
wagon, its hoops standing like barren ribs, the
cover rolled up in the bed of the wagon with the
heavy load of cooking gear and supplies, flour and
sugar, baking powder, dried apples—and most of
all, plenty of coffee.

Shad Blankenship stood leaning relaxed against
his own saddled horse and eyeing Jameson quizzically. He trimmed a thick shaving off a plug of
Lorillard tobacco and shoved it into his mouth.
His breath already had a sweetish tobacco smell,
and a trickle of brown worked into the rusty beard.

"What do you think of the layout, Shad?"

Shad never had been one to mince words. "I
think that if a marshal was to come snooping
around, about two-thirds of this crew you hired
would drown theirselves tryin' to get across that
river. What jailhouse door did you prize open?"

"I wanted them tough. They won't stampede
back to town the first time we run into an Indian
with the paint on."

Shad shrugged, still not liking it.

"Well, there's one of them ain't goin'. He got in a
little argument last night and didn't have a sharp
enough knife. Other feller just naturally gutted
him. Shows what kind of an outfit *we* got."

Jameson swore under his breath. One man lost
and they hadn't even started yet.

Shad said, "We'll have to watch them like

hawks or first thing you know some of them are liable to run off with our stock.''

Jameson was still troubled about the man they were short. ''I figured you and me are strong enough to handle them.''

Put that way, there wasn't much Shad could do except sourly nod assent. ''I reckon.''

Despite the early hour, despite the chill which still penetrated the men's light coats, a good-sized crowd of onlookers gathered. This expedition had aroused a lot of comment. Most people agreed it was foolhardy. Jameson would be so busy fighting Indians he couldn't hunt buffalo.

He'd had poor luck finding men who would hire on. He didn't try to get any of the Miles and Posey men, for he felt that would be unfair to the company. Besides, C. T. Posey wanted to send them out for one last attempt up against the edge of the northern treaty territory. Jameson had managed to get three men who had worked for Miles and Posey a little in the past. They weren't what he wanted, but they were all he could get.

Then Ransom King came to his rescue and rounded up a crew for him.

''These are good men that'll take you down there and bring you back,'' King had said. Then he had reflected a moment and added, ''Maybe *good* isn't just the right word. *Tough* is more like it.''

Now Jameson pointed his chin toward the crowd of onlookers who stood around and watched. ''They'll do a lot of thinking, Shad, sitting around here doing nothing. Then they'll get the fever. There'll be other outfits down there by winter, unless I miss my guess.''

Shad observed, "It'll be a good thing we was the first."

Jameson gave him a dig in the ribs. "That's what I've been trying to tell you all along."

C. T. Posey came striding up, chewing rapidly on his cigar. If anything, he was more nervous than Jameson.

"Look at me," he said, holding out his hand. "Quivering like a whipped pup and not even going."

He rubbed the palms of his hands on his trousers. "Everything looks good, Gage. You won't have to worry about the military. Won't be a patrol across your route in two days."

Jameson glanced at Shad Blankenship, grinning. It never ceased to amaze him how Posey could know what was going on at Fort Dodge. The army was supposed to keep hunters from working south of the Arkansas. But it was a careless hunter who couldn't slip past the soldiers. It was as if a tacit agreement existed between the hide outfits and the officers at the fort.

He remembered what Colonel Dodge had said when J. Wright Mooar asked him about heading south. "Boys, if I were hunting buffalo, I would go where the buffalo are."

It was almost universally agreed among the plains army officers that destruction of the buffalo was the quickest way to peace. The reservation looked good to a hungry Indian.

Ransom King rode up to them mounted on a fine big sorrel with three stocking feet. Jameson hadn't seen the horse before and stopped to admire its good lines, the deep heart girth, the strong legs that could carry a man all day and not give out.

King nodded at Jameson, then said to C. T. Posey, "What did you think of those hides, C. T.?"

Posey replied, "I thought they were plenty expensive."

King threw back his head and laughed. Presently he said to Jameson, "My wagons are ready, any time yours are." His gaze swept down Jameson's line of wagons and to the extra horses and mules bunched at the lower end.

Jameson said, "We're about ready, I think. I've already lost a man, and the wagons haven't turned a wheel."

King nodded. "Heard about it from some of my crew. Fool got in a fight over a poker game. Just a five-dollar bet, that's all it was."

Jameson started walking down the line of wagons, leading his horse and making a last check of each wagon as he passed it. The wagons contained primers and gunpowder and lead, corn and salt and everything else it would take for a long hunt on the prairie. Jameson reasoned that as the hides stacked up, the supplies would diminish and make room for them.

"Mighty little to die for, five dollars," he mused to King, who rode slowly beside him.

"Lots of people die over money," King replied lightly. "What else *is* worth dying for, when you boil it down? But if I ever do it, it won't be over any measly five dollars."

Jameson frowned. That was a mighty narrow way of looking at life, the way he saw it. Or death either.

A woman pushed through the crowd and stopped in front of it, holding her long gray coat tight at the throat, not caring that her slender ankles showed amid a swirl of petticoats.

"There's Rose," Jameson said, "wanting to tell you good-bye."

King nodded, resignation in his face. "I'm glad I'm getting to do it. I'm bored to death with her."

Jameson smiled. "If I had to die, that's the way I'd want to do it, bored to death by someone as good-looking as that."

King shrugged. "Well, I gave you the chance. You didn't take her."

He started to pull away, toward Rose. He turned back to say, "I've thrown my extra animals in with yours, and my wagons will drop in behind when yours lead out. See you later, down the trail."

He moved his horse out and swung down beside Rose.

Jameson rode back to the head of the line. A lean, long-legged man strode toward him in the dawn, wearing faded old army clothes, carrying a rifle in his hand and a heavy roll of bedding over his shoulder. It was the skinner, Messick. Dropping the roll in the street, Messick leaned the rifle against it and raised his hand in greeting.

"Mornin', Gage."

"Morning, Nathan."

Messick glanced over Jameson's wagons, where everything seemed to be ready to travel. "I want to go with you."

Jameson said, "I didn't aim to steal anybody from Miles and Posey."

"You ain't stealin' me. I just quit. I've worked

with you so long, Gage, there ain't anybody else I can get along with."

Jameson smiled, glad to have him. Messick never was one to add any cheer, but with a man like him in charge of the hides there wouldn't be any spoiled goods. "Hop up on a wagon, then. We're fixing to roll."

Messick pitched his bedding up onto the chuck wagon, shoved his rifle under the seat, and climbed up beside the little cook. The cook nodded at him, clenching the whipstock in one hand, the lines and the coils of his rawhide whip in the other. Two thin men, one short, one uncommonly tall.

Shad Blankenship rode up to Jameson, rocked back in the saddle and spat a stream of tobacco juice at a lanky gray dog which nosed around a wagon wheel. Then Shad's big black dog charged up and put the intruder to flight, trotting back with a grand air of self-importance.

Shad waved his hand at the line of wagons. "All set, Gage."

C. T. Posey was there, too. He held out his hand, and Jameson bent down to take it.

"I envy you in a way, Gage," the hide buyer said. "I never saw this country the way it used to be. I'd like to see it, just once in my lifetime. But I'm smart enough to know my limitations, and you have none. Best of luck to you."

"Thanks, C. T."

Then Jameson pulled away and looked back at his long string of wagons, the stamping mules, the impatient men.

"All right, Shad. Let's take them to Texas."

5

ANGLING SOUTHWESTWARD, he didn't try to push the wagons hard the first day. With untried mules, untried wagons and untried men, it was better to take it easy and watch. By the time he reached Crooked Creek late in the afternoon, he had seen half a dozen mules and at least a couple of men he probably should have left in Dodge.

Too late now to do much about it. He had other mules he could put into the teams. But he was stuck with the men.

Shad Blankenship rode up to him and pointed to the creek. "Pretty good camping spot over here. Want to pull up the wagons?"

"Not till we get across. I get nervous on the wrong side of a creek or river. Spent too many days watching them flood and wishing I'd gotten across them when I could have."

Shad argued, "This one ain't fixin' to get out of banks. Ain't a cloud in sight."

"Call it a policy. We're crossing it anyhow.

Normally it was an easy crossing. It would have been this time, except for the nigh leader on the chuck wagon. He had been kicking and fighting all day. When the cold water splashed around his legs, he came in two.

The pots and pans, buckled on the chuck box, set up a clatter as the wagon began to jerk. The cook cracked a whip over the mule's ears and swore in language such as Jameson had seldom heard before, a careless mixture of the most profane of both English and Spanish. Jameson grinned, wondering how a man so small could have so powerful a voice.

The mule kept pitching and kicking, getting his forelegs over the neck of the animal beside him and stirring the whole team into a frenzy. They whipped the wagon back and forth at the water's edge until it began to rock.

The thin, bewhiskered cook began looking for a way to get off, but it was too risky. The moment he jumped, the well-loaded wagon might tip over on him.

Jameson spurred back across the stream. Plunging in next to the mules, he grabbed the reins up close and wrapped them around his saddle horn, pulling the nigh leader's head hard against his leg. He half dragged the reluctant animal across the stream. By the time he got him out on dry ground the mule had stopped fighting. But it was rolling its eyes and dancing about in the traces.

Breathing hard, Jameson said, "He needs to be worked till his belly drags—work the foolishness out of him."

The cook was still talking to himself. "Needs a

good dose of hickory limb right between the ears, that's what he needs. I thought for sure I was fixin' to get me a bath in that cold water.''

Jameson began to see humor in it then. He couldn't help but think that a bath wouldn't have hurt the young cook much. But he had found that some of the best hide-camp cooks never washed anything but their hands. That much Jameson demanded.

He had tried this cook's handiwork in Dodge before he hired him. Now, in the first night camp, he knew he hadn't made a mistake. The cook was a short, thin Texan named Pruitt—''Reb'' Pruitt they called him, because he had been in the army of the Confederacy. He was thirty or thereabouts, with a deep browned skin and an irresponsible growth of whiskers that made him look much older. He had come up the trail to Abilene with a couple of thousand Longhorn steers and a salty bunch of Texas cowhands. The way Jameson heard it, he had been in some sort of scrape down there and couldn't afford to return to Texas—not the settled parts, anyway. So he'd been cooking for the hide outfits.

Homesick, he had seized upon the chance to see his native state again, even though it would be only the buffalo plains, a couple of hundred miles from any settlement—or any law.

After Jameson had dropped his tin plate and cup into a washtub with the rest, he called the men together. Old Shad Blankenshp stood beside him as he counted them. Ransom King and his small crew stood in the background, listening.

The little Texas cook rattled the tinware as he

washed it in the tub, and he grumbled constantly to himself. But he was listening, too.

"I've called you together in a bunch," Jameson said, "because there's a thing or two that needs saying. I want them said right at the start, so no man can claim he didn't hear them.

"There aren't any tenderfeet in this outfit. I chose you on purpose because you all knew something about the hide business. There's not a man among you who hasn't fought Indians, so I don't think the sight of a feather or the smell of gunpowder is going to run you off. But if you think it might, I want you to say so right now.

"It's one thing to loaf around Dodge and talk brave. It's another to belly down in the grass a thousand miles from home and try to get some Indian before he puts an arrow through you. Anybody who wants to turn back can do it right now, and no hard feelings. But after today, there won't be any turning back. Not for me and not for you. We're going down into Comanche country, and we're not coming back till every wagon is loaded with hides.

"Now then, is there anybody that wants to leave?"

The cook had stopped rattling the tinware. Jameson stared hard at the silent faces, one by one. Not a man moved. He hadn't thought they would.

The utensils began to clatter again.

"The next thing," Jameson went on, "is the Indians. Now we're not going down there to fight. We're going down there after buffalo hides, and that's all. We'll go a long way to get out of a fight if

63

we have to. A battle is too costly, even when you win it. You always lose men and you always lose stock. Wagons aren't any good to us without the men to load and handle them or the stock to pull them.

"We're bound to run into Indians. But there won't be any shooting unless it has to be done. If they act friendly, we'll treat them accordingly. If they're hostile, we'll try to keep out of their way. We'll fight only as a last resort.

"So I don't want any itchy trigger fingers around here. If any man gets us in trouble needlessly . . . I'll shoot him."

He paused a moment, studying the faces as that soaked in. He wasn't sure exactly why, but he cast a glance at King's man Trencher.

"The last thing," Jameson said, "is about the hides. They're mine. I'm paying you well for skinning and stretching and for handling the mules. But every so often somebody gets a notion he can make more by stealing hides and stashing them away for himself.

"Well, it won't work here. I know that most of you aren't wearing any halo. But I don't care what you've done in the past as long as you shoot straight with me.

"In the first place, there'll be no way for a thief to come back and get the hides. In the second place, I'll be keeping a good tally of the buffalo killed and the hides we stack up. If I ever catch any man trying to steal from me, he'll wish the Comanches had him."

The cook had stopped washing the utensils and sat staring at Jameson, the wash water dripping from his fingers. Only when Jameson turned away did he go back to his job. And he had stopped grumbling to himself.

Jameson walked out to where his bed lay on the ground, still rolled up. He sat down wearily.

A heavy silence hung over the camp awhile, and uneasy silence as the men weighed what he had said. He could feel the resentment from some of them. It had been strong talk. But it had needed saying.

Finally he heard the riffle of cards and someone saying. "Who's game for a little poker?"

Jameson leaned back against his bedroll. He had brought a few tents, but they wouldn't be used while the weather was still good. He enjoyed sitting in the open, watching the stars brighten against the darkening sky.

Shad Blankenship stuffed his stinking old pipe with tobacco and lighted it with a burning stick from the Texan's dying cook fire. He flopped down beside Jameson and puffed silently on the pipe. Shad chewed tobacco all day, but at supper he always spat out his quid. He customarily lighted up a pipeful of tobacco and smoked it out before crawling into his blankets.

Shad took an awl from his pocket. With it he carefully began to worry a diagonal hole through the end of a big lead rifle bullet. Jameson watched him with curiosity as the old man finished one and blew the lead shavings out of it, wiping it slick on the leg of his trousers. Shad put that one in his pocket and started on another.

"What's that for?" Jameson asked him finally.

Shad held the second one up and eyed it critically. "That there is a squaller."

"Squaller? Never heard of it."

"Man told me about them last spring. Says they work pretty good."

"What're they for?"

"Maybe I'll show you sometime, before we get off of this trip."

Jameson knew there was no use prodding him. Shad would tell him in his own good time, if he wanted to. Or he might not do it at all, for he could be as contrary as an old bear.

Shad fixed up four or five bullets with the holes in them, then put away the awl. Presently he glanced at Jameson, puffing the pipe.

"Some of them Sunday-school boys didn't much like it, you puttin' it to them so blunt. But I reckon you'd just as well square off with them right at the first. You ain't exactly got a camp meeting here, and they ain't no deacons."

"It's a hard life, Shad, and it takes hard men. Think I can handle them?"

Blankenship drew deeply on his pipe. "You *got* to."

They had breakfast over with and the mules all hitched to the wagons by daybreak. All of them, that is, except the nigh leader on the chuck wagon, the same knot-head that had come so near to turning the wagon over in the creek. With a lightning-quick flick of his hind foot he dealt the cook a glancing blow to the left leg that sent him spinning.

So angry he couldn't even cuss, the cook tried to get up, fell, tried to reach the mule with a whip, couldn't, and finally grabbed up a handy rock and heaved it at him. It missed.

Jameson ran to the man. He knelt down and carefully felt of the leg.

"Doesn't seem to be broken. Need somebody to drive for you?"

Pruitt got his voice back and exercised it well, showing a wide range of vocabulary. Then he said, "All I need is the loan of your buffalo gun and one cartridge."

Jameson wanted to smile, but he didn't. Seldom had he seen such magnificent anger.

"I'll take that mule out of the traces and throw him back with the loose bunch," Jameson offered.

The cook considered that, then slowly shook his head. "No, leave him where he's at. I'll get a right smart of pleasure popping his rump with a whip every time he wiggles an ear."

Two teamsters finished harnessing the cook's team for him while Jameson helped him up into the wagon seat. Pruitt rubbed his leg tenderly.

"Come noon," he said, "it'll be blacker than the ace of spades."

He picked up his heavy rawhide whip with a certain fondness and fixed a baleful eye on the mule. "Ready, anytime."

They moved out without further incident, and things went well enough until past noon. About two o'clock Shad Blankenship motioned Jameson up to the lead and pointed toward a rise in the prairie. Jameson squinted. It was a long way off, and at first he thought it was a couple of antelope, watching the wagons in their great curiosity.

But Shad Blankenship had the eagle-keen eye of a man who'd been dodging Indians for forty years.

"Cheyenne," Shad said. "They been watching us quite a spell."

"Hunting party?"

The old man grunted and shrugged his shoulders. "More than likely. But then an Injun will hunt for a good many things besides game, you give him half a chance."

Jameson looked back at the wagons, not liking the way they were straggling out. He didn't think anybody else had seen the Indians yet. He reached down for the reassuring feel of the saddle gun under his leg. He had left the heavy Fifty in one of the wagons.

"I'll ride out and have a look," he said. "You better get those wagons pulled up close together. Have them ready to circle in a hurry."

Shad moved to comply, then pulled up short and pointed back to the rise. "You don't need to ride out. They're comin' to us."

Suddenly the two Indians had multiplied to twenty-five or thirty, moving down toward the wagons. Not fast—just an easy walk—easy and determined the way only an Indian could be.

"Powwow, looks like," Jameson said. "But pull those wagons into a circle, just the same."

By now others had seen the Indians, and the word passed back down the line like fire crackling through the cured dry grass. Gun barrels glinted as the men on the wagons prepared themselves. The stock tender quickly shoved the spare horses and mules in close. At Shad's signal the wagons began pulling into a circle, the stock inside.

King spurred his horse into a lope. Flanked by his hulking man Trencher, he pulled to a stop beside Jameson.

"War party?" he asked. Jameson saw no excitement about the man, nor a trace of fear. King was as cold as the waters of the Arkansas in January.

"Hunting party, I imagine. But it could turn into a war party if they like the odds. We can't let them come into camp."

He noticed the way Trencher deliberately drew his saddle gun from its sweat-caked scabbard. No need to check the load. It would always be loaded. Trencher's eyes were hard, eyes that enjoyed looking down the barrel of a rifle at an Indian. Or maybe at anybody.

Jameson said, "Go easy on that rifle."

A sudden defiance flashed into Trencher's gray eyes, as if to say: I'm King's man, not yours.

Jameson spoke evenly, "What I said last night goes for you too."

King reached across and touched Trencher's arm. "He's the wagon master. Listen to him."

Trencher nodded resentfully. He wasn't a man who liked to be ordered around. Jameson had an idea he would as soon tell King where to head in as he would anybody else. And King more than likely would knock him flat on his back.

The Indians stopped a couple of hundred yards from the wagons. The leader made some show of handing his weapons over to the braves beside him so the white men would know he was coming in unarmed.

He was Cheyenne, all right, a warrior of some years, obviously a leader of standing. He rode in slowly, proud, arrogant, dark eyes touching each man briefly, then somehow picking Jameson as the leader. He was looking at Jameson as he reined up twenty feet short and swung his arm in an arc, pointing northward. He did it twice, and there was no mistaking what he meant by it.

You're over the line, he was saying in effect. You're on forbidden ground. Go north, to your own treaty lands.

Jameson shook his head negatively and pointed south. He swept his hand toward the wagons and again pointed south.

Even at the distance, he could see anger flare in the old warrior's black eyes. The Cheyenne pointed at his own chest, then northward, and said something.

Jameson looked at Shad, puzzled. "He's trying to talk English."

The Indian tried it again. "*So-ja. So-ja.*"

Shad spoke. "He said 'soldier.' He's trying to say he's fixin' to fetch the soldiers."

Trencher lifted his rifle. "He ain't bringing no soldiers."

Jameson's pistol leaped into his hand.

"Trencher!" He let the man hear the deadly click of the hammer.

Trencher lowered the rifle. His eyes seared Jameson, and there was murder in them. Then he roughly jerked his horse around and spurred back toward the King wagons.

King said, "Trencher's got a head like a rock."

Without patience, Jameson replied, "You remember the agreement. Either he takes orders from me or he leaves the outfit.''

"I'll talk to him, and he'll take orders. I'll need him, later on.''

The Indian had sat solemnly watching it all. His eyes had widened when Trencher brought up the rifle, and his hands had lifted on the rawhide reins tied to the lower lip of his paint horse. But he had made no move to run.

To Shad Blankenship, Jameson said, "You speak Cheyenne, and I'm poor at it. Tell him we want to treat with him. Tell him there's no need for the soldiers.''

It took Shad four times as many words to get it into Cheyenne, and he made much use of his hands, Indian style. The Indian replied, talking for at least a minute. It took Shad only seconds to put it into English.

"He says we're south of the treaty line in Cheyenne hunting grounds. Says the buffalo is scarce enough without us makin' an extra swath through them. Says get, and get fast.''

"Tell him we've got gifts for him. Tell him we're passing through his land without killing any buffalo. Tell him we're going across the Cimarron to the Staked Plains, into the Comanche country.''

Shad translated that, and Jameson thought he could almost see a smile on the old Indian's face. The Cheyenne talked for two minutes.

Jameson eased a little. "I thought he might be happier if we promised him gifts.''

A spark of laughter came into Shad's pale eyes. "It ain't the gifts made him grin. It's that we're goin' into the Comanche country. Says this is one bunch of buffalo hunters he won't have to worry about again."

Jameson winced. The man who said Indians had no sense of humor didn't know much about Indians. But occasionally their jokes got a little too close to where a man lived.

King guffawed. His sense of humor was as bad as an Indian's, Jameson thought sourly.

"Go get him some tobacco, Shad," Jameson said, "and a little sugar."

Blankenship brought these things and handed them to the Cheyenne. The old warrior received them with dignity. He began talking again. In a moment Shad turned back to Jameson.

"Says this ain't much. Says the white men killed most of the buffalo, and his braves' bellies are empty. Says ain't we got somethin' for his men?"

Impatience stirred in Jameson. They hadn't killed any buffalo yet. How could they furnish meat for all these Indians?

He heard a stamping of hoofs and the squeal of fighting mules. He looked back toward the wagons, straightening as an idea hit him.

"Tell him yes, we've got something for him. Just wait a little."

Quickly Jameson rode to the chuck wagon.

"Pruitt, hand me a piece of rope." He signaled a couple of men to come to him. "Help me unharness this mule, then go get another one out of the loose bunch to take his place."

Bob Pruitt came close to smiling as Jameson put a loop around the cantankerous nigh leader's neck and pulled the harness off.

Jameson led the mule back and handed the rope

to the chief. The old Indian made no effort to hide his delight at this tasty gift. His smile didn't even break when the mule stretched its neck, teeth gleaming, and tried to bite a chunk out of the paint horse.

The Cheyenne wished them a good trip over the Cimarron, then led his unwilling prize away.

Jameson signaled the wagons to move out again. And as the chuck wagon came by, a new mule in harness, the little Texas cook said:

"Jameson, I reckon you're a fair to middlin' kind of a Yankee after all."

The Cimarron!

For years Jameson had heard of it. Now he was seeing it for the first time as it quartered its way slowly down across the plains.

It wasn't much to look at here, the banks sandy, almost flat. Dried salt glistened on the ground far beyond the present bounds of the river, showing where it overflowed during its occasional sudden floods. The river itself was two hundred yards wide, maybe closer to three.

"Looks shallow enough to wade," he spoke as Shad Blankenship pulled his horse up beside him and looked down at the reddish water which moved sluggishly through the sand.

"Don't fool yourself," Shad said. "There's a heap sight more to this river than meets the eye. She's quicksand, all the way."

Jameson knew. He'd heard a lot about this river. Its deep bed was filled with sand. Through it moved a treacherous undercurrent which dragged down the unwary. He had seen other quicksand streams filled with the rotting corpses of buffalo which had been bogged down and had died there, helpless. Men said this one was the worst of all.

"We'd better hunt us a crossing," Jameson said.

While the wagons waited, he and Shad moved up the river. A few hundred yards away they found an old, well-beaten buffalo trail leading into the water. He looked up at Shad.

"You seldom go wrong, following the buffalo trails."

"Maybe," Shad said. "But there ain't no crossing safe forever. The sand moves around."

Jameson spurred into the water. Within fifteen feet of the bank he could feel the drag of the quicksand on his horse's feet. The bay felt it, too. He moved quickly, nervously, not letting his feet stay in one place long enough to get caught. Jameson rode him all the way across, Shad following.

Gaining the far bank, Jameson reined up to let his horse breathe.

"Not too bad," he said. "We need to pack it some."

On the other side again, they signaled the wagons up to the crossing. Then they went for the extra mules and horses.

"We'll put them back and forth across, six or eight times," Jameson said. "Pack the bottom down so the wagons can get over easier."

By the time the horses and mules had splashed across the muddy river for the last time, the bottom was as solid as Jameson could ever hope for it to be. They unhitched the doubled wagons and took them across one at a time. The chuck wagon was the first to go.

Reb Pruitt popped his whip at the team. The mules hit the water, splashing mud over the Texan as he cursed them on. Only once did the wagon slow down. The whip popped and sang, Pruitt standing up in the bed of the wagon, his lusty voice reaching clearly across the river. In moments the wagon had gained the far bank and pulled up, the dirty water trailing back to the river in deep ruts the iron rims had left. Pruitt pulled up far out of the way and proceeded to make camp.

The next wagon rolled in, and the next, and the next. When half of them were over, the mules were brought back and hitched to the trail wagons.

When all had finished the crossing, Jameson sat his horse on the bank and looked back at the angry boil of red mud which bled slowly down the river from the line where the wagons had gone over.

Shad Blankenship swung down beside him and stretched his weary legs. "Life's full of river crossings of one kind and another, seems like. We've put a tough one behind us, Gage."

Jameson nodded and faced back around. He looked south across the great reach of open, rolling plains. From here on, they would have little to go by. There were no maps, no descriptions other than the vaguest kinds.

Ahead of them now lay the Llano Estacado, the Staked Plains, the great unknown land. Anglos had probed at the edges of this great mystery, but few had penetrated deeply into it. None were known ever to have gone completely across.

Far, far to the south lay the settlements of Texas. To the east strung the great dusty cattle trails over which millions of Longhorns were being trekked northward to the shining new ribbons of steel. To the west huddled the ancient adobe villages of New Mexico.

Yet here in the center was this vast tableland of buffalo grass, stretching on and on, dreaded because it was unknown. Unknown because none had yet had the heart it took to try it. Even the army had left it alone. Most of the maps still left it blank.

A few went so far as to say why. A few said the word that really explained: *Comanche!*

Gage Jameson looked southward into the edge of this great land and felt a chilling awe come over him. He knew he was going where few white men had ever gone. He might see land no white man's eyes had ever seen.

Never before in his life had he felt so alone, had he felt this tingle that moved up his spine as he looked southward into the forbidden land. He had crossed the Cimarron. Somehow he knew that something had changed. Nothing would ever be quite the same again.

6

SOUTH OF THE CIMARRON, then across the narrow neutral strip. And one day Jameson knew they must be in Texas.

Already he had begun to see a difference. Here the grass did not grow tall and rank as it had in Kansas. He had heard tell of this great turf of short grass stretching down across the Texas plains like a huge rolling carpet. Hardly more than boot-top high, the dry leaves curling like thin wood shavings—buffalo and mesquite grass, with a strength unmatched by the taller feed to the north. And it had a little longer to go before winter too, because this was farther south.

He stepped out of the saddle and poked with the toe of his heavy boot at the cured brown grass. He kneeled and felt of it and looked up keenly at Shad Blankenship.

"Been a good while since it rained, you can tell that. And the summer has been plenty hot down here, I'd bet my boots. But look how much green this stuff still carries at the base.''

Shad nodded. ''Sure, she's a real buffalo country, Gage. That's why they like to drift south come fall. Grass down here stays strong through the winter—don't dry up and go weak like broomstraw. You mark me, young'un, there's gonna be buffalo enough down here for everybody.''

So they moved on south, the iron wheel rims leaving the dry grass broken and crushed to the ground, the trails stretching out behind like endless ribbons. Gage Jameson rode far out in the lead, topping every rise, his eyes searching eagerly for the distant black dots that meant buffalo grazing out across the plains.

But he didn't see them. Always there were buffalo chips, some not long dry. In places great concentrations of the shaggy beasts had grazed the grass down almost to the ground. Everywhere there were the deep corduroy buffalo trails, often dozens of them running parallel, only feet apart.

But now the buffalo had gone.

Three days the wagons lumbered slowly along, the crews breaking camp late and setting up again early in the afternoons, while Gage Jameson, Shad Blankenship and Ransom King scattered out to scour the prairie, to search up and down every creek and header they could find. Each evening the riders followed the wheel tracks into camp and dismounted stiffly from tired horses, their faces telling the other men without need for words. There weren't any buffalo.

Firewood was scarce on these long stretches of grass, even up and down some of the little creeks.

Reb Pruitt began using wood only to kindle his fires, then kept them going with dried buffalo chips.

"Some deal," the Texan laughed, raking the fire and adding the fuel that was a staple of the plains. "We come after buffalo hides and all we find is buffalo chips."

But if it was a joke to Pruitt, some weren't taking it that way.

Jameson could feel the restlessness among the crew even before the complaints began. The first he heard was from a man named Tully, one of the three old Miles and Posey men he had been able to hire. It wasn't meant for his ears, but he heard it anyway, from the off side of a wagon.

"The boys was beginnin' to say he was jinxed that last trip out. Maybe they was right. He never found much buffalo then. He ain't finding any now. There's plenty of sign—we've all seen it. But where's the buffalo?"

Jameson made no reply—didn't even let the men know he had heard. Out in camp this way, they always tended to gripe when things weren't running to suit them. A man had to expect it.

But the fact that they were talking began to rowel him. He rode harder, looked a little farther each time he went out.

Then one day, along with the buffalo sign, he found something else. Horse sign, and a lot fresher. Unshod horses, a couple of them with ragged hoofs badly in need of a trimming. He followed them a way, coming at length to a creek lined with hackberries. There the men had dismounted to drink and water their mounts. The footprints remained plain in the mud. No heels. No straight-edged leather soles. These had been flat-bottomed moccasins, the toes tending inward.

Comanches.

In camp he told Shad Blankenship. Shad just nodded his rusty head.

"Seen it yesterday. Found an antelope they'd put an arrow in and took the guts and a hindquarter from."

"Why didn't you tell me?"

"No use getting the camp all stirred up. Anyhow, you knowed there was gonna be Injuns before you ever started." A flicker of humor showed in Shad Blankenship's sharp old eyes. "I thought we was huntin' buffalo."

Impatience prodded Jameson. Shad's idea of a joke would be a scalp-hungry Indian catching a bald man.

"I want to know about the Indians, anyway, in case they decide to start hunting *us,*" Jameson retorted.

It was a hunter's paradise, if the hunter had anything besides buffalo on his mind. Every day Jameson spotted antelope grazing in scattered bunches. At sight of him their heads would bob up, and off they would go in a flash of broad white tails. They would run awhile, then stop upon a rise and look back at him, standing in single file like a string of Indians, poised to run again if he angled their way.

Then there were the lobo wolves, bigger than most dogs, ranging far out from water, preying on jack rabbits and prairie hens and anything else that didn't get out of their way, watching all the while for buffalo or other large animals that might be lamed or mired or somehow at a disadvantage. Their slashing fangs could bring down a full-grown buffalo, with their superb teamwork and just a little luck.

Along the creeks Jameson saw quail, mink, skunk and raccoon, and on one timbered stream, beaver.

It seemed to him that he had never in his life seen anything quite like it. Here in the brown weeks before the onset of winter, these high Texas plains seemed to be reaching their peak. The grass was cured. The game was fat and sleek, putting on hair for the cold times not far distant. The prairie and its teeming life drowsed under an autumn sun that had lost the sullen scorch of summer but still possessed a gentle and loving warmth.

A wonderful country, Jameson thought.

But where were the buffalo?

Taking care of the livestock was the biggest problem he had, for here on the Llano Estacado lived the best natural horse thieves ever born. With so many horses and mules, hobbling and sidelining every one of them at night would be a monumental task. Instead, he circled the wagons, putting the horses and mules inside the circle for protection against the rare skill of the Comanche.

A sudden low growl almost at his ear snapped Gage Jameson out of a sound sleep in the middle of the night. He sat up straight, shoving back his blankets and grabbing at the six-shooter under his pillow. A gentle hand touched his shoulder.

"Quiet," Shad Blankenship whispered. "The old dog says there's somethin' out yonder that don't belong."

Blankenship's shaggy black mongrel, almost invisible in the pale moonlight, growled in deep-grained hatred.

Jameson held his breath, listening.

All he could hear was the gentle night breeze with its autumn chill, searching restlessly among the wagons. That, and the dry rumble deep in the throat of the big black dog.

Shad Blankenship sat rigid, listening too. But Jameson knew Shad couldn't hear anything. Age had sharpened his eyes, but his hearing wasn't what it used to be.

The dog suddenly stiffened, hackles rising. Jameson sank to the ground, looking in the same direction, trying to see some movement against the sky. He waited a long moment, hardly breathing. Then he caught it—the form of a man crouched low, stepping slowly, carefully, almost straight at the wagon under which Jameson lay. He saw the slant of a feather.

Indian. Jameson wondered how many more there were.

The dog's growl went louder. The Indian stopped suddenly, hearing it.

There was not enough light for good aim. Jameson drew back the hammer, aimed by instinct, and squeezed the trigger.

With the sudden crash of the gun, mules and horses jumped, hoofs clumping excitedly on the thick turf of grass. Men burst out of their blankets, yelling. Other guns sounded, the racket echoing off into the night as men fired at shadows and at the wind whispering through the grass.

After a time all went silent again. Men settled down to watchful waiting. Some few even crawled back into blankets and went to sleep again. But most were awake for good, talking nervously in low voices if they talked at all.

Shad Blankenship was as calm as a stock pond on a still day. He stretched out on his blanket, unworried. "I reckon they got as big a scare as we did. They won't be nosing around any more to-night."

"Wonder how many there were?" Jameson mused. "I only saw the one."

"Ain't any tellin'. Maybe just a lone buck wantin' to steal him a horse and make a good showing back in camp. Or maybe a whole passel of them hoping to catch us asleep and leave us afoot. What difference does it make now?"

"Lucky thing that dog of yours smelled them coming."

Blankenship snorted. "Luck, is it? You didn't think I kept that shaggy old monster around for his looks, did you? Wasn't for him, they'd have laid me out in the grass a long time ago."

Jameson grinned, the tension leaving him. "Well, from now on I don't care if he looks like Lucifer, just so he keeps on hating Indians."

Best they could make out next morning was that four, maybe five Indians had attempted the raid on the stock. Spots of red in the dry grass proved that Jameson had at least winged a would-be horse thief.

Ransom King came out to look over the sign.

"From now on," Jameson told him, "we'll keep two men on guard at all times, in one-hour shifts. With the stock inside the circle, and that black dog around, we shouldn't have any trouble."

King frowned. "Maybe all the trouble won't be from the Indians."

Jameson looked sharply at him. "What's that supposed to mean?"

"There's a lot of loose talk drifting around the camp. They're saying, some of them, that you're not ever going to find any buffalo. They're saying they don't mind Indian risk when they're skinning hides and making money. But they're not getting any hides."

With a nettle of anger Jameson said, "What do *you* think, King?"

King smiled quickly. "If I didn't believe in you, I wouldn't have joined you with my wagons."

Sometime that night someone shook Jameson's shoulder. He sat up quickly, reaching for the pistol, thinking the Indians were back. But it was a hide handler named Ludlow, a silent, morose, black-bearded man who never mixed with the others, always stayed to himself.

"I think some of the boys has shucked the harness, Jameson," he said. "Tully is gone. I don't know how many of the others."

Jameson stood up angrily, throwing aside the blankets.

"Tully had guard duty just before me," Ludlow said. "He was supposed to wake me up when it come time to relieve him. He never did."

"There was another man on guard. Where is he?"

"One of Tully's buddies. He's gone too."

Jameson stomped out into the wagon circle. "Everybody up!"

As the men gathered in the darkness he mentally counted them off. Three gone. Tully and the other two old Miles and Posey hands.

It was too dark to check the livestock, but Jameson knew within reason that they had taken a horse apiece. Saddles too, and he had few of those. He saw his own bay hunting horse standing nearby and felt relief that they hadn't gotten him.

The rest of the men knew now what had happened. He could not tell by their faces whether they were considering trying the same.

Shad Blankenship watched Jameson closely as the anger played in his face. "Nothin' you can do about it now, Gage. They're gone.

Jameson said in a brittle voice, "We're *going* to do something. If we don't, some of the rest may pull the same stunt."

He crawled back between his blankets, but he didn't sleep any more. At the first paling of the night sky he was up and punched Shad awake.

"Roll out, Shad. I may need those eyes of yours."

The cook got up, too. Yawning and scratching and talking incessantly, Pruitt soon had coffee boiling for them, and a bait of antelope meat was ready by the time the two saddled their horses. Jameson impatiently wolfed his down, swung into the saddle and spurred out.

Shad, a slow eater, caught up to him after awhile. Jameson was moving into a long-reaching trot, sometimes in a lope, his grim eyes following horse tracks in the grass. The thick turf kept the hoofs from cutting into the ground much, but the brittle grass, broken underfoot, made a trail a man could read.

All morning they rode, slowing down to save the horses when it became clear that they weren't going to make a fast catch. Sometime past noon Jameson began to regret his haste in eating breakfast. Hunger commenced to tug at him. The long ride over the unchanging prairie had drained the anger from him, leaving only a stolid determination. He would catch those men if he had to ride all the way back to the Cimarron.

Presently Shad reached back into his saddlebags and brought out a little bundle done up in oilskin. "Cold biscuits and meat," he said. "Good thing I come. You'd have starved flat to death."

Jameson grinned then, relaxing from the grimness that had held him.

They stopped at a little stream and watered and rested the horses. Impatience prickled Jameson, but judgment told him to wait. Though he could push himself till he dropped, he couldn't ever afford to overpush the horses. He sat and drummed his nervous fingers on his boots, while Shad Blankenship lay so relaxed that Jameson couldn't tell whether he was napping or not.

Presently they were on the go again, pushing as hard as they dared. Along late in the afternoon, Jameson reined up and squinted at something far ahead.

"What does that look like to you, Shad?"

Shad stared, his eyes narrowed against the sun, the reddish brows knitted up close. "It's them.

They're restin' by that creek yonder."

Jameson waited a moment before he moved out, looking for a way to ride in close without being seen. He reined the bay around, riding back the way they had come until he passed down under a rise and well out of sight. Then he angled westward, crossing the creek and coming up in cover of underbrush.

Near the quarry, the two men reined in to study the situation closer.

"Asleep, I think," Shad whispered. "All three of them. Must've rode half the night and all day. Horses about give out, I reckon, and the men too. If we was Comanches we could get us three juicy new scalps."

"Not looking for scalps, Shad. I just aim to get them horses back."

Dismounting, they tied their own horses. Saddle guns in hand, they eased forward. The creek was shallow, the water not reaching quite to the tops of Jameson's black boots as they waded across. The leather was so heavily greased that little of it would seep through.

The two were within twenty yards of the sleeping men when one of the horses suddenly raised its head and whinnied. Tully jerked erect, blinking and feeling desperately for the rifle that lay beside him.

"Don't touch it," Jameson said evenly. "Just stand up there and leave it alone. The rest of you the same."

The other two were awake now. One glared at the other. "Thought you was gonna keep watch."

"Shut up," Tully barked impatiently at them.

Then to Jameson he said sullenly, "All right, so you caught up with us. Now I guess you're taking us back."

"No," Jameson said, "I don't want you back. I don't want to have to watch you all the time we're out."

"Then what did you trail us for?"

"Those horses. They're mine."

The runaways stiffened. Tully licked his dry lips. His voice lifted. "Look, Jameson, this is the middle of Comanche country. You wouldn't set a man afoot out here, would you?"

"You'll have your guns. And you're halfway to the Cimarron already. Walk all night and hide all day. You can be in Dodge in a couple of weeks if you get high behind."

Tully's eyes were frightened. He looked down at his rifle on the ground, then up at Jameson, but he didn't dare make the try.

"Pick up their guns, Shad," Jameson said. "We'll carry them with us a ways, then drop them off."

The men looked around them at these endless plains which reached on into infinity. They were awesome enough to a man on horseback, but they were terrifying to a man afoot. Jameson could see dread settle over the runaways like a black shroud.

A hollowness was in Tully's voice. His eyes pleaded. "Jameson, this is the worst thing you could do to a man."

"Not quite," Jameson replied flatly, without pity. "Hanging's rougher. That's what horse thieves generally get."

He waited until Shad brought up their horses.

Mounting, he started to push the three runaways' mounts southward again. Then he stopped just long enough to untie canteens and sacks of supplies from behind two saddles and let them drop to the ground. He gave them this gesture of mercy, and this one only.

After they had ridden awhile, pushing the three horses in front of them, Jameson dropped the guns to the ground and looked back. The three men trailed them at a walk, a far piece behind. They wouldn't get to the rifles in time to use them.

Shad Blankenship grinned. "I been worried all day what you was gonna do when you caught up to them. I was afraid this morning you was fixin' to shoot all three."

"This morning," Jameson said flatly, "I was mad enough to."

It was well past midnight by the stars when Jameson's instinct led him to the camp, and he saw the red glow of campfire coals, kept barely alive by the succession of guards. They turned the horses loose. Then, before he did anything else, Jameson walked around the camp, grimly counting the men rolled up in their blankets.

Ransom King sat at the remains of the campfire, drinking black coffee which Pruitt kept on the coals all night for the guards. He didn't get up as Jameson and Shad approached wearily. He sat there, watching.

Jameson poured himself a cup of coffee, and Shad followed suit. Jameson sat on his heels, his eyes touching Ransom King. King silently studied him awhile before he brought out the question. The way he said it, it wasn't really a question at all.

"You fetched back the horses but no men."

"They won't be coming back."

King's eyebrows arched, and in the firelight his gaze dropped to Jameson's gun.

Jameson said, "I didn't shoot them. But by the time they walk all the way back to Dodge, they may wish I had."

King poured the dregs of coffee out into the grass, pushed to his feet and stood there, some dark humor seeming to stir him.

"You've got a soft streak in you, Jameson. *I'd* have shot them."

He walked off into the darkness, toward his wagon.

Shad Blankenship watched him disappear, then commented, "He would have, too. He's got it in his eyes."

Jameson nodded. He remembered the fury in King's eyes that night the man had rescued him in the Dodge saloon. He knew King could catch afire as easily as he could break into wild laughter.

Jameson finished his coffee, letting it drive out the chill the night air had settled upon him. Then he crawled into his own blankets. But he didn't sleep. He lay awake, listening, watching.

Sometime up in the morning Shad Blankenship's snoring broke off. He lay quiet a little, then raised up on one elbow.

"You ain't ever been asleep, have you?" he said, frowning.

Jameson shook his head. Weariness was stone-heavy on him, but worry was heavier.

There was a little of admiration in the old man's voice, and admiration didn't come lightly to Shad

Blankenship. "Then sleep. Nobody is fixin' to slip away this far up in the mornin'. Anyhow, I'll watch. It don't take much sleep for an old man."

Jameson hadn't expected the men to like the way he had set the runaways afoot. He wasn't much surprised, then, when at breakfast he felt the hostile eyes of some of the crew upon him. They didn't say anything. They didn't have to. But he could smell revolt in the air, just as he could smell a faint hint of winter in the dawn wind.

He ate in silence, counting those men he felt might side with him, and the count didn't come to much. Only two men were left with whom he had ever worked—Shad Blankenship and Messick.

Looking at Reb Pruitt, he mentally gave him a question mark. This small, thin man was a good cook, and Jameson had an idea he was a scrapper from way back yonder in spite of his flapping jaw. But Jameson was a Yankee, and so was the rest of the crew. He didn't think Pruitt was going to get worked up much over any kind of a fight between Yankees. More likely he would sit on his hands and grin as he watched it.

He glanced at the hide handler Ludlow, that brooding, heavy-bearded man who sat to himself now as he ate. He made friends with no man, and he never spoke except when it was necessary to the work.

Jameson shook his head. No, he didn't think Ludlow would help him, either. There would be no one except Shad Blankenship and Messick. And maybe Ransom King. Maybe. . . .

One thing certain, Jameson couldn't afford to get out of sight of the camp. It was his conviction that most of the crew—maybe all of it—would appropriate horses and mules and head north the minute he was gone over the hill.

"Shad," he said, "I've been trying to keep north, so we wouldn't have so far to go if we were forced to run for it. But now I'm pointing them south, across the Canadian. We'll find buffalo if we have to drive all the way to the Rio Grande."

Jameson allowed himself to ride as far ahead as he could without letting the wagons drop back out of his sight. They crossed over the sandy Canadian, fighting its treacherous undercurrent much as they had done at the Cimarron. Then they pushed on south, angling a little westward.

Long days came and went, and long nights in which Jameson slept little or not at all, trusting hardly anyone any more. Bone-weariness and the lack of sleep sank his eyes back deep beneath his brown, put an aching slump in his shoulders. But he kept on riding, kept on watching the men, kept on looking for buffalo.

In camp at evening the men gathered silently around a poker game that started as soon as supper was over and lasted far into the night. Almost invariably the winner was the man who promoted the game, a short, fat little skinner named Blair Farley, a man with a loud, quarrelsome voice and thick, stubby fingers which were amazingly efficient with a deck of cards. His greedy eyes seemed able to read a man's thoughts. Already his pocket was stuffed with IOU's against half the wages the men might expect to earn on this expedition—if they found buffalo.

This too was making the crew surly, knowing that much of their pay already was gone. It added to the charge of tension that slowly built up in the camp.

Sometimes even Shad Blankenship's eyes turned longingly to that poker game.

Then one day about noon Jameson heard a shout and blinked quickly at a movement atop a promontory half a mile southward. Shad Blankenship had ridden out on a scout. Now he came spurring his dun horse, the dust rising behind him.

One thought raced to Jameson's mind. Comanches. He reached down for his saddle gun and at the same time yelled to the men on the wagons.

"Look sharp. It may be trouble."

But it wasn't trouble. Shad eased up on the speed as he loped in. He drew rein and stopped the heaving horse just in front of Jameson. A wide grin cut across his dusty, red-bearded face.

"We've found them, Gage," he said excitedly, loudly enough for the men to hear him. "They're over that hill yonder and down the valley, a million of them. We've found the buffalo!"

7

THE WEARINESS seemed to lift from Jameson's wide shoulders and the burning tiredness from his blue eyes as he stepped stiffly off his horse atop the hill. He gazed down the creek with its scattering of big cottonwoods, its banks lined with smaller timber. His look moved on out across the level prairie where not a mesquite or sagebrush blocked the view. His pulse quickened.

There they were, the buffalo, scattered in small grazing bunches as uncountable as the stars in a crisp night sky, fly-specks out yonder as far as a man could see. They brought up bittersweet memories of old days on the Republican and the Arkansas, times that had vanished with the high-plains wind.

There were bunches of cows, many of them trailed by big stocky, glossy calves, blackish brown now after shedding the reddish hair of their first months. Some calves grazed alone, already weaned. In among the cows he could see young

spike bulls, not old enough yet to challenge the big
bulls for mastery, not ready to take their place as
sires. The older bulls grazed separately now, in
little groups of three or four to as many as twenty.
Breeding season was over.

Far out yonder amid the specks of black, Jameson saw a band of antelope, and a big gray timber
wolf sneaking along looking for the crippled or
sick, the buffalo warily eyeing him, an occasional
bull tossing his head threateningly.

Jameson watched a pair of old bulls in a buffalo
wallow, rolling in the dust, digging in with their
horns and throwing dirt high over their backs with
their massive heads, trying to drive away the buffalo gnats.

Presently the wagons came. Men walked to the
top of the hill to gaze out upon the sight. The threat
of rebellion had disappeared like a wisp of smoke.

No one shouted. No one jumped up and down.
Men stared silently or swore softly to themselves.
They stood there a long time as if they couldn't see
enough of it, as if they had never seen buffalo
before. Even the somber Ludlow, who had never
shown any emotion except an everlasting contempt for his fellow man, softened and smiled a
little, squatting on the grass and unconsciously
whetting a skinning knife against the black leather
tops of his high boots.

"You men just stay here and look awhile,"
Jameson said. "Shad and I are going to hunt a good
place to make camp."

The creek flowed in a northerly direction, emptying into the Canadian somewhere above. The
two men rode southward toward the head of it.

Bands of buffalo grunted and scattered away from water. The animals would run off a way, then stop and turn to look back with their tiny weak eyes, water dripping from the long stringy beards that sometimes almost dragged the ground.

"Ain't got much fear for a man on horseback, have they?" Shad commented. "Ain't been choused much—maybe none at all."

Jameson nodded in satisfaction. "That's a hopeful sign. Means the Indians haven't been hunting around here."

Jameson picked a flat spot high up enough from the creek bed so that a sudden rise of floodwater wasn't likely to wash away the camp, yet close enough so that water-carrying would not become burdensome. A few big cottonwoods there would spread shade over the men working in camp during the heat of the autumn afternoons. Smaller timber would provide fuel for the fires and poles for the rough, semipermanent corrals that would take the place of the wagon circle in protecting the stock at night.

Jameson saw more buffalo grazing upwind along the creek.

"Shad," he said, "you go bring the wagons, I'll try to get us some fresh meat."

He slipped the saddle gun out of the scabbard, circled around downwind of the buffalo and came up behind them. When he was close enough, he let them see him. They started down the creek toward the camp site, shuffling along in a trot. He picked out a nice fat cow which either hadn't had a calf this year or had already weaned it so she could store up flesh to carry the next calf already conceived within her. He let her pass on through the camp site so there wouldn't be any lingering smell from the butchering.

When she was about right, he spurred in and fired at her from the saddle, aiming at her lungs. The second shot slowed her, and the third brought her to the ground. He stepped down from the horse, dropped the reins and moved up. Taking care that she didn't thrash her head and catch him on those sharp curved horns, he stepped in with his thick-bladed ripping knife and cut her throat to bleed her and lessen the risk of spoiling the meat.

Soon the wagons arrived. The crew began setting up camp, unloading gear, emptying several wagons which would be used to haul fresh green hides back to camp as the kill got under way.

Messick and another skinner set to work on the cow Jameson had killed. They slit through the jawbone first and took out the tongue. They ripped the hide up the belly and skinned out the legs past the knee. With their curved skinning knives they began to lay the hide back away from the flesh, working from the belly downward toward the back bone on one side, then straining together as they turned the heavy carcass over to skin out the other. Normally they would hitch a pair of mules to peel the hide off once they got it started. But this kill was for meat, and the hide under the carcass would help to keep it clean.

Jameson put the other men to work chopping posts and poles for corrals and digging holes to set the posts in.

With a purpose before him now, something there that he could see, he no longer felt his weariness. Having something to work for gave him new wind and new will. He walked back and forth through camp a hundred times, making plans, directing work, pitching in where it wasn't going fast enough. When it looked as if the corral job was moving along satisfactorily, he walked out to the flat area downwind of camp, the hide-drying and stretching ground. It had to be cleared of tree limbs, dead stumps and other obstructions.

By dark the fence posts were up. The poles hadn't been laid between them, and there wasn't time now before night. But long ropes tied to the posts made a handy enough substitute for one night. Maybe tomorrow. . . .

He flopped down across his bedroll, savoring the good dry smell of burning wood and thinking he would rest awhile before supper.

When he awoke the sun was coming up red on the cloudless eastern horizon. Someone, Shad of course, had spread blankets over him to protect him from the night chill. He pushed them back and grinned sheepishly at the old man who sat cross-legged, studying him with amusement in the glow of dawn light.

"Thanks, Shad."

Shad made a "forget it" motion with his big old freckled hand. "You look a heap sight better this mornin'. Got them black satchels out from under your eyes for a change. Think you're ready to shoot some buffalo?"

"That's what we came for."

The hump steak from the fat buffalo cow, he thought, was the finest he'd ever sunk a tooth in.

Ransom King walked over and sat down beside

him as he finished breakfast. King was already shaved. He wore clean clothes, although they were rumpled from the trip.

"I'm ready to do some shooting this morning, Jameson, if you are."

Jameson nodded. "We'd better pick our hunting grounds so we won't be shooting at each other. Shad and I will go south this morning. Why don't you work north, down the creek?" He looked at King's rifle and saw that it was a Sharps like his own.

"We'd better learn the sound of each other's guns," Jameson said. "Maybe it'll be important some day, if we hear guns that don't belong to us."

King said, "Good idea. I'll do my own shooting, as far as I can. If my skinners get to catching up with me too fast, Trencher can help me bring down a few."

They waited around camp, helping finish preparations, until Jameson's big pocket watch showed it to be nine o'clock. There was plenty to do.

"Let's get started, Shad," Jameson said finally. "They ought to have grazed by now."

With bellies full of the strong grass and the morning sun getting warm, the buffalo would settle down, stop moving around. Listless then, they were less likely to scare away at the roar of the big guns.

Jameson slipped on his coat with the deep pockets that held extra shells. He fastened the cartridge belt around his waist, every one of the thirty-two loops holding a loaded cartridge. Shad Blankenship did the same.

"Never have taken a good look at that gun of

yours, Shad," Jameson said. Shad handed it to him. It was a Sharps Forty-five, a fourteen-pounder with a thick octagonal barrel that could stand the heat of a lot of firing. Jameson rubbed his hands over its smooth finish and read the two words imprinted deeply on the left-hand side of the breech, *Patented 1869*.

"Used to carry a Fifty, didn't you?"

Shad grunted. "Used to be young, too. But for a man of my age, this fourteen pounds turns to forty soon enough. I just got to get a mite closer sometimes, that's all."

The wagons followed them, drawn by four mules apiece. Two mules could do it, but a man never could tell what might be over that next hill in strange country. Four mules in a run could pull a heap faster than two.

In half an hour the two horsemen rode part way up an eminence, far enough so that they could easily see over it. A couple of hundred buffalo were scattered under the brow of the hill, some still grazing a little, most of them full and resting, already chewing cuds, lying with noses to the wind.

"Fair chance of a good stand down there for both of us," Jameson said, and the old man nodded.

Jameson didn't need to wet his finger and stick it up to get the drift of the breeze. It was out of the northwest and had been all morning. They rode back down from the point and eased a little farther south, so the breeze blew from the buffalo to them.

The skinners crawled out of the wagons and squatted in the grass, patiently sharpening their ripping and skinning knives on the steel that each man carried on his belt. One man drank water from a five-gallon keg that was wrapped in a piece of old woolen blanket, wet to keep it cool. Here the men would wait, out of the way, until the shooting was done.

Blair Farley was already shuffling his cards, trying to promote a time-passing game.

There was nothing to tie the horses to, but nothing was needed. They had been trained to stand where the reins were dropped. Jameson and Shad left them and walked directly up the side of the little hill. Pausing a moment at the top to look the situation over, they started down again on the other side, walking carefully, directly at the buffalo.

It was a peculiarity of the buffalo that he paid little attention to a man afoot, especially if the man walked straight at him. Jameson thought it was probably because the buffalo could detect little motion that way, his eyes being weak and sometimes half grown over with thick hair. Many times Jameson had walked up within rock-throwing distance of buffalo before they began to shy away. On horseback he could never have approached so close.

Two hundred yards from the buffalo, Shad said quietly, "About far enough. Too close the first time and they're sure liable to scatter."

Carefully, making as little motion as possible, Jameson sat down, taking off his cartridge belt and laying it on the dry grass before him where he could easily reach it. He removed the coat and laid it out where he could get to the extra cartridges in the pockets and keep the belt loops full. He laid down his canteen, which he might have to use to cool the barrel.

He looked at Shad, seated six feet from him so they wouldn't be in each other's way. His eyes asked, "Ready?" and Shad nodded.

There was usually a leader in any bunch. If this leader moved away, the others would follow him. Without him, the buffalo generally stood around in confusion. There never was any sure way to know which one the leader was. For that, a man had to depend on instinct.

A big cow was looking around suspiciously, her nose in the air, testing the breeze. Jameson eased down to a prone position, setting up the rest stick over which to lay the heavy barrel of the Big Fifty. He studied the breeze, thought he knew how much to allow for it. He shoved the cartridge into the breech, took long, deliberate aim, held his breath, and squeezed the trigger.

The deep roar was enough to set a man's ears to ringing. The cow jerked violently and began backing up, slinging her head. He had missed the target, he knew. He had shattered her jaw. A few more seconds of this, throwing the blood around that way, and she would stampede the whole bunch.

At the heavy boom of the gun, the other buffalo shied. Those which had been lying down jumped up, front end first. But they didn't run. They stood in confusion, not knowing what was happening, not seeing any enemy.

Jameson aimed and fired again, correcting his windage. The puff of dust just behind the cow's shoulder was right where he had tried to hit her.

She squatted back, hind legs going limp. She swung her head from side to side, then lay over heavily, kicked a time or two and sank slowly into death, her little black eyes staring into nothingness.

Shad Blankenship squeezed off a shot. Another buffalo staggered a step, then fell.

Jameson looked up and saw the black smoke of the gunpowder rising, drifting off into the gentle wind. On a still day a man could nearly suffocate himself in smoke with a Sharps. And no joke about it, he could deafen himself eventually, exposing his ears to the roar of the big guns year in and year out.

They settled down to shooting them, taking their time to keep from overheating the guns, yet wasting no time either. Nearly every shot bagged a buffalo, although sometimes it took an extra bullet or two to dispatch one. Instead of running, the other buffalo would look on in bewilderment. After the first few shots, they stopped shying from the roar of the guns. A few even lay back down, losing interest in the strange noise and going back to chewing their cuds.

"Good thing we got a little breeze," Shad said quietly. "Keeps them from gettin' the blood smell."

At length an old cow began to move away, and it looked for a moment as if the rest of the bunch would follow, breaking up the stand. Jameson drew a bead, allowing more windage for the long shot because she was at least four hundred yards away. The first shot stopped her momentarily, sent her squatting. But she got up again and began to move once more, dragging a little.

Jameson thought the stand was lost. Then she stopped and turned sideways, looking back as if to find her hidden assailant. Shad's rifle roared at the broad target. The dust puff from the brown hair was just where it should have been. She went down and stayed down.

Jameson looked at the old man in admiration. "Did you ever miss a shot in your life?"

"Once. Didn't eat for four days, either."

After awhile, lying still in the sun, Jameson could feel sweat work from under his hat and trickle slowly down his dusty face. It burned his eyes. When he rubbed them he got gunpowder in them from his hands, and that made it worse. His shoulder ached from the recoil from the big rifle.

He could feel the intense heat from his heavy gun barrel and knew it needed to cool anyway. Opening the breechblock, he picked up the canteen and poured water down the muzzle, jerking his hand away from the scalding steam. When the barrel had cooled some, he pushed the corner of a greased patch into the eyelet of his wiping stick. He ran it into the barrel and worked it up and down to break loose the accumulation of burned powder.

He laid the rifle down to let it cool off. Already he could count some thirty buffalo lying dead or dying on the ground. Shad Blankenship was still shooting, waiting as long as two minutes sometimes between shots. He wasted precious little powder.

It had always been a puzzle to Jameson why the

buffalo would stand and take this murderous fire instead of stampeding away. They nosed curiously at the fallen, and now and then a cow hooked at one of the dead. Each time one acted as if it had begun to get the scent of blood, Shad or Jameson brought it down.

For two hours the stand held up, the band of buffalo slowly diminishing. At last the surviving animals commenced to get the blood scent, and then they broke into a run.

"Want to follow them up, Gage?" Shad asked. "They'll settle down in a little while."

Jameson shook his head. "I reckon we've done enough killing for now."

He stood up and walked out among the fallen buffalo. He flinched at the sight of the dead, glassy eyes, the bloody mouths and noses that resulted from the lung shots. Here and there a buffalo still breathed, still kicked. Those Shad and Jameson saw, they finished with their pistols.

Flies already were buzzing around the dead, expecially those shot earliest, where the blood had crusted and turned black.

Shad Blankenship shook his head. "A bloody business, Gage. Man has to get himself a hard stomach to stay in it, and there's few that really enjoy it."

"I never have, Shad. In a way, it doesn't hardly seem right. God put them here, and I expect He had a good reason. Now we're killing them off as fast as we can skin them."

Shad shrugged. "It's a business. About the only one left any more. A man didn't do this, he'd just about starve to death. If we don't shoot them, somebody else will. It's gonna be done, regardless."

Jameson nodded. "It's *got* to be done. It's a bloody job, but I don't reckon it's any worse than killing cattle in a slaughterhouse, except for the waste. And there's not much we can do about the waste. It's too far to market for the meat.

"And as long as there's buffalo, there'll never be any settlement. They feed the Indian and keep him fighting. There's no room for the farmer where the buffalo graze. There's no room for the cowman, either. It's a question of which we're going to have, the buffalo or the settler. When you look at it that way, it's not much of a question, is it?"

They signaled the skinners, who brought up the wagons. Each skinner moved along, testing the sharp blade of his knife across the rump of a fallen cow. If she quivered in reflex, she wasn't quite dead and he moved on to another. If there was no movement, he set right in to skinning.

Shad and Jameson climbed to the top of the hill and sat down there to watch the operation, and to keep an eye out for Indians that might have been drawn by the gunfire.

Shad bit himself a fresh chew of tobacco.

"Funny thing, ain't it? We talk all the time about civilization, and how do we get it? By killin', that's how. I first come out here, it was the beaver. We trapped beaver so the high-toned boys back East could sport them a beaver hat.

"Of course we weren't lookin' ahead. All we bothered about was makin' money. But what was really happening, we was gettin' to know the country. We was opening it up for them that was to come later. When the beaver trade folded, some of us started scouting for immigrant trains and surveyors and one thing and another, and we was shootin' game to feed them. Then the hide trade started, and we commenced to killin' the buffalo.

"And all the time we was killin' the Injuns, too. Killin' so we could have civilization. Some way to get it. Like a marshal I seen once, come to settle down a wild town. Slams his pistol down on the bar and he says, 'We're gonna have peace around here if I have to kill every one of you to get it.' "

Shad shook his rusty head. "And what happens to us old hands then, when civilization does come? We don't fit in. We brung it, but they got no place for us. We wind up in jail, or beggin', or livin' off the county. I seen many of them old mountain men thataway, just drunk theirselves to death. They'd destroyed the only kind of life they could fit in."

Jameson put his hand on Shad's patched knee. "There'll always be a place for you, Shad, as long as I'm around."

Shad looked him straight in the eyes and said, "How do you know there'll even be a place for *you*, Gage?"

8

THE AUTUMN weeks drifted by, the skies of an evening taking on that deep horizon-line purple that meant winter was nearly here. The hair on the buffalo became thicker now. Before long there would be good robe hides that fetched an extra price.

The hunting was all a man could want. Always the drying area was covered with a patchwork of hides, sometimes stretching two hundred yards along the creek. Each day the wagons came in off the hunting grounds loaded with fresh hides green and heavy, sticky with blood and undried flesh. The handlers pitched them down and spread them out upon the ground, dusting them with poison to keep the bugs away. Then they would stretch them on the grass with the hair side down, securing them by pounding pegs down through tiny holes slit in the edge. Here the hides would stay for three or four days, sometimes five or six now that the autumn's daytime heat had largely waned. When well dried, they would be turned over, hair side up. Finally cured, these flint hides would be loaded upon one of the wagons and lashed down, their space on the drying ground given up to fresh hides just coming in.

"Doing mighty well," Jameson said to Shad Blankenship late one afternoon, watching the handlers peg out forty green hides from that day's shooting. "Never saw hunting grounds stand up any better."

"Me neither," Shad agreed. "Only moved camp twice, and then just a little ways up the creek so we wouldn't have so far to hunt and pack hides. Wouldn't be surprised if we're in Dodge before Christmas."

"You getting ready to go back, Shad?"

Shad pondered a moment, then darkly shook his head. "No, to tell the truth, I ain't. You know what always happens to me when I get to town. This is where I belong at. Even if it *is* a messy job, and a man gits sick of the killin', sometimes I wish I never had to go back. Wish all this would never change."

He turned to Jameson, melancholy in his pale eyes. "What is it gets into a man, Gage? Even with all the blood and sweat and dirt, this is a heap sight better than being in town, drinkin' that swill they sell for whisky, chokin' to death on tobacco smoke while you're losing everything you own in a crooked poker game. What is it gets into a man and sends him runnin' back to town like an ox to the slaughter, ready to take his whippin' again? Why is it a man don't ever have no better sense?"

Jameson shrugged. He didn't have an answer to

that. He needed one himself.

Every time he left town, he fully intended to stay out until it was absolutely necessary that he return, and then to stay only long enough to pick up new supplies. But good intentions weren't enough. Now, already, he was beginning to get that restless itch, to start picturing Dodge in glowing colors. He didn't want it to be that way. He wished he could change it. But there it was.

If only he had him something to tie to. . . .

Shad nudged him. "Yonder comes Ransom King and his wagon."

Jameson watched, nodding. "A good hunter, Shad. He's a crack shot. He can put a bullet in a buffalo about as handy as anybody I ever saw."

"Yeah, and seems to enjoy it, too. Ever watch him when he's got a stand? Shoots for all he's worth. Somethin' takes hold of him, and he loses that nice smile. Worries me sometimes he'll burn up his gun barrel. And when the buffalo run, he jumps on his horse and takes out after them. Strings them out sometimes for a mile or two. Like a kid on a picnic."

Jameson commented, "Gets a lot of buffalo."

"And makes the rest of them so wild you can't get in a mile of them on horseback."

King rode in beside his skinners' wagon and dismounted, a little stiff from the ride. He watched distastefully as they pitched the day's green hides onto the ground. A big drop of half-congealed blood splashed off onto the leg of his trousers.

"Dammit," he shouted in sudden anger, "watch what you're doing."

Quickly he slapped at the blood with his hands,

trying to get it off. Then he rubbed his hands together, scowling darkly at the smear of drying blood on them.

Shad said quietly, "Some of the polish is comin' off now, and the brass is beginning to show."

Even in camp Ransom King managed to stand a head taller than anyone else in appearance. He was the only man who shaved every day without fail. Even Jameson didn't try to do that. Often Jameson and Shad threw in when the work was heavy, skinning hides or moving them around. But King always found someone else to handle the dirtier details, avoiding the stain that stamped other men with the brand of their trade.

Seeing Jameson and Blankenship, he moved toward them, leading his horse. He had his laughing days and his black days. This was a black one. There was no dash or fun about him. He still scowled. He wiped the dust and sweat from his face with a clean handkerchief.

"Durn this business anyway."

In a light voice, trying to ease King's dark mood, Jameson remarked, "I always thought you liked the hide business. The excitement and shooting . . . selling your hides and counting your money."

King shoved the handkerchief back into his pocket. His mouth twisted as he watched his men spreading out the hides. "The shooting, sure. I like the feel of a gun in my hand. Always did. Like the feel of power it gives you. But the rest of it. . ."

His eyes narrowed, and he cursed under his breath. "My stomach turns over every time I get the grease and blood of them on me. And the smell, Jameson, it sticks to a man like death. Get so I hate the sight of the lousy monsters. I'll be glad when the last one is dead and rotted."

Jameson looked at him questioningly. "For a man who hates the business, you've done mighty well at it."

"The money, Jameson, the money. You'd be surprised what-all I can stand if there's enough money in it."

There hadn't been any trouble during these weeks, nothing a man could rightly call trouble. Once a handful of Indians had tried to work up to the corral in the dead of night and get off with some horses and mules. But Shad's old black dog stopped that, just as he had done before.

The only other trouble was King's man, Trencher.

He had been busy enough at first so that he wasn't much bother to anyone. But later, as camp routine got old, he started getting restless. He began sitting in on Blair Farley's poker games and losing steadily. His IOU's to Farley were mounting up. Trencher sulked around, his eyes narrowed and mean, looking for a chance to stumble over someone's feet.

One night Shad Blankenship was busy tarring a wagon hub and spat a stream of tobacco juice without much attention to where it went. Part of it splashed on Trencher's boots, already thoroughly stained by mud and blood and buffalo grease. Roughly Trencher grabbed the old man's thin shoulder and spun him around. He wrapped his fingers in Shad's short beard and jerked Shad's face up close to his own, so hard that the tears came to Shad's eyes.

Jameson saw it from afar and came running. But he didn't need to. Shad raised his boot and stomped down hard on Trencher's instep. Then his knee came up sharply, and Trencher doubled over in agony. Shad slapped him across the face with the tarbrush, leaving a heavy black smear. He planted the sole of his boot firmly on Trencher's hip pocket and roughly sent him sprawling under the feet of a mule.

Startled, the mule began to jump and kick. Trencher scrambled away on hands and knees, haste making him look ridiculous.

Shad's black dog piled in on him to make it worse, his long teeth seeking blood. Shad called him off.

Men who had seen it started to laugh. But when Trencher stood up, scowling and dusting himself, his furious eyes stabbing at them through the smear of tar, they shut up. He turned back to Shad, crouching a little.

But Shad stood his ground, his big fist clenched around a wrench. The dog was growling, black hair standing stiff.

"By Judas Priest," Shad said angrily, "I was gougin' eyes and bitin' ears before you was ever weaned. Next time you come at me, bucko, you better have you a doctor handy."

For a moment they glared at each other. Shad didn't give an inch. Presently Trencher turned and stalked away. From then on, he never came at Shad again. He often eyed him from a distance, a goading hatred in his heavy face. But he always gave Shad plenty of air.

"I reckon I handled that." Shad's words were

clipped in lingering anger.

"I reckon you did," Jameson agreed worriedly. "But you better watch your back from now on. Trencher looks like he'd have the memory of a bull elephant."

Blair Farley had been watching, hands tucked into the waistband beneath his heavy paunch. Jameson motioned him aside and said sharply, "You caused this, you and those poker games of yours. Cause me any more trouble like this and I'll let you walk back to Dodge!"

"It ain't my fault if Trencher's got his dander up," Farley replied in a whiny voice that grated against a man's nerves.

"No? Well, I'll tell you something else that had better set you to thinking. You haven't got a friend left in camp, Farley. Most of them hate you because you've been winning their money. We're a long way from town. We ever get in a scrap with Indians, what's to keep somebody from potting you during the excitement? Then nobody would owe anything."

He saw fear strike in Farley's eyes. "You don't think somebody would?"

Jameson shrugged. "You know these men. What do you think?"

Farley walked away, visibly shaken by a thought that never had come to him before. Jameson heard someone ask him about a poker game, and Farley turned it down.

Later Jameson spoke to Ransom King about Trencher. King listened, frowning in thought. "I'll let him shoot a few buffalo," he said. "That's all he needs. Let him kill something and it drains that meanness out of him for awhile.''

Jameson shook his head wonderingly. ''I guess you know him. But you've got a mighty peculiar taste in helpers.''

''I don't pretend to like him, Jameson. He's crude and he's mean. But I can handle him, and he's a good man for the job he does. As long as I make money, I can tolerate anything or anybody.''

Came a time when the buffalo were thinning. The bunches were so small now that Jameson and Shad never got to hunt together any more. They separated, each taking a wagon and his own skinners, trying only to keep within the sound of each other's guns. There had been some Indian sign lately, and Jameson's eyes constantly searched the skyline.

Shad said, ''Been the time of year the Comanches like to go south and raid the settlements. That's maybe why we ain't seen much of them. But they'll be back here for the winter.''

One day after Jameson had killed enough buffalo for his skinners to have an afternoon's work, he sought out Shad Blankenship and found him already through, sitting on a rise watching his men.

''Let's go hunt a new camp site, Shad, one where there'll be more buffalo.''

They set out up the creek. There were buffalo, all right, but badly scattered. They rode ten miles, maybe twelve, and finally reached the rocky head of the creek, where a strong stream of cold, clear water burst forth from a fissure in the rocks to form a year-round spring.

Up here were more buffalo. Jameson liked the

idea of camping by the spring. It was a good place, with lots of hackberry, stunted elm, and most of all the big cottonwoods. In places the buffalo had rubbed the trunks almost slick getting rid of the spring-shed hair, with its itchy lice and ticks. Even after all these months, a tuft of shed hair still stuck, here and there.

Shad Blankenship was worried.

"Look at them buffalo," he said, "turn tail and run quick as they see us. They ain't been so wild back down the creek. These buffalo has been hunted, Gage. Hunted on horseback."

"Indians, you think?"

"What else? Maybe we better have us a look around."

They skirted the spring and eased southward. Presently Jameson pulled up short, tilting his head to listen. "Shad, did you hear something?"

Shad shook his head. "Gettin' so deaf I can't hear thunder."

Gage listened a little, finally stepping down and dropping the reins, standing free of the horse so not even the squeak of the saddle would keep him from hearing. The sound grew. It was like thunder. But it rolled steadily, without a break, gradually swelling louder. Soon Gage could feel the ground begin to tremble a little beneath his feet.

"Stampede," he said sharply. "Buffalo stampede!"

His heart quickened. He stepped back into the stirrup and swung up, automatically looking about him for a place of escape and seeing little but the rolling prairie, the stream, the spring—nothing that would stop a crushing tide of buffalo.

"We've got to make a run for it, Shad," he said. "Let's get over that rise yonder so we can see how they're heading. Maybe we can get out of the way before they get here."

They spurred up over the rise. Even before they reached the top Jameson could see the cloud of dust that rose into the plains sky. Then he saw the buffalo coming fast, directly toward them.

"Lord," Shad breathed, "must be ten thousand head."

They were fanned out over a half-mile front. Jameson's bay horse was fidgeting nervously, wanting to run. Jameson felt his own pulse pounding.

"That way, Shad," Jameson shouted, pointing. "Maybe we can get past the edge of the herd before they run us down."

He spurred then, spurred hard, and the bay horse answered with speed. His long legs reached out. Jameson knew this was the payoff for his having bought a horse of strong body and strong lungs. Behind him he could almost feel the breath of the buffalo on the back of his neck. It was the movement of air set in motion by the surging body of the stampeding herd. Beside him Shad was leaning over in the saddle, talking to his dun horse, urging him to more speed.

Jameson looked back once at this thundering black sea of buffalo that would pound horse and man to powder if ever they made a misstep, if ever they fell in the path of this living avalanche. He saw the bobbing black heads, the black eyes, the little streams of saliva that trailed from the mouths of the running animals. He could feel the fear that swept the buffalo, that kept them surging forward, and it became his own fear, swelling in his chest, choking off his breath.

Little by little the spurring riders worked toward the edge of the herd. Some of the leaders were even with them now, running along beside them. Jameson looked back often, gauging how much farther they had to go, already feeling the power begin to play out in the big bay horse beneath him. He kept urging the horse on.

And finally . . .

"We're clear, Shad!"

They pulled up then to let the herd roar past them. A rush of wind and dust whipped their faces. The horses danced fearfully, still strung high from the long, hard run.

In a little while the herd had gone on past. Down there somewhere the buffalo would run themselves out, and they would settle down to graze again, as peaceful as if nothing had happened.

"Reckon what tetched them off?" Shad asked, trying to rub the dust from his watering eyes.

"I've got a sneaking idea," Jameson replied. They trotted their horses a little, easing them down to a walk, cooling them gradually.

The sound of the stampede faded away and there was nothing left to show for it but a wide swath of trampled grass and a lingering of stifling dust that slowly drifted out on the easy breeze.

Now Jameson began to hear something else.

"Shooting, Shad. And I thought I heard somebody yell."

Shad's eyes narrowed. Presently he heard it, too.

"Coming from somewhere across that hill yonder," Jameson said.

Dismounting and leading their horses, the two men cautiously worked up the hillside. They dropped the horses' reins and crouched as they neared the top, keeping low to present as little silhouette as possible. Shad Blankenship dropped to his belly.

"Look yonder, Gage. Ever see such a sight in your life?"

Down there a large group of Comanche warriors, stripped to breechclouts and all mounted on good horses, had driven a group of buffalo into a mass. Now they circled them, the dozens of hoofs churning up a billowing cloud of dust to drift away with the wind. Most of the Indians loosed arrows into the herd as rapidly as they could restring their bows. Now and again, as a buffalo made a rush to get out of the surround, a warrior charged after him with a lance. Those few Indians who had rifles were using them principally on the animals which broke into a run.

Jameson was glad he had brought the binoculars out of his saddlebags. He raised them to his eyes and watched a lancer lope up behind a running buffalo, holding the lance across his body, the off end the highest, his knees tucked under a rope wound around the horse's body. When he had gained the position he wanted, he thrust downward with the lance, shoving it hard, then pulling it out again as the buffalo faltered. The lancer pierced the animal a second time, pushing in and holding the lance until the buffalo went down.

He saw a bowman ride in close and loose an

arrow at a running bull. As the missile drove home, the buffalo turned sharply, heading into the horse, sending it rolling. The Indian scrambled to his feet, grabbing his fallen bow and what spilled arrows he could snatch off the ground. In desperation he sent arrow after arrow into the charging animal, so rapidly Jameson lost count. The buffalo went to its knees, still hooking at the Indian. The warrior walked back to his horse, carefully looked him over for injuries, then remounted and returned to the slaughter.

Not a single animal escaped the Comanches.

Now the fun was over and the work part began. Other Indians materialized out of a brushy draw to start the skinning, the butchering of the meat. Jameson watched, fascinated, the skilled hands of the red men.

These were the Comanches, savage, brutal. Yet truly they were children of the land, nomads, akin to nature and the creatures in a way the white man could never be, following the rains, following the grass, following the buffalo.

Shad nudged Jameson. "This ain't the girly show at no fancy dance hall, young'un. They find out we're up here, we're liable to put on a little show ourselves."

"I wonder where their camp is," Jameson mused, still watching through the binoculars.

"It don't matter to me. I ain't been invited and don't aim to go."

Jameson grinned at him. Shad wasn't scared. But he had the deep-grained caution that had kept his hair on through forty years of dodging Indians.

Jameson said, "I've got a notion to trail them, at

least far enough to locate their camp. I'd rather find it now than stumble on it some day by accident.''

The wrinkles deepened in Shad's ruddy face as he narrowed his eyes, looking down upon the Comanches. ''Whatever you say. You're the wagon master. We better step soft, though. Me, I'm an old man, and I've lived out a full life. But you're still owin' the house.''

The Indians brought up pack horses. Rolling the meat in the fresh hides, they loaded it onto the horses and headed out, leaving little but scattered patches of blackened blood to show where the slaughter had taken place.

''Don't waste much, do they, Shad?'' Unlike the white man, Jameson thought.

Shad shook his head. ''Winter coming on, they can't afford to.''

It wasn't hard to follow the Indians. It wasn't as if the Comanches were trying to hide their trail. Up here, in the middle of their stronghold, they probably had no thought of any need to do so. Riding slowly, his eyes squinted, nervously searching out the skyline and every patch of brush as they rode along, Jameson could feel the flesh crawl up the back of his neck. His mouth was dry, and he constantly licked his lips. But he kept riding, and he kept watching.

''They ever see us,'' Shad Blankenship spoke softly, ''she's gonna be the biggest horse race you ever saw.''

Jameson nodded, his hand tight and sweaty on the reins, his knee pulling in for the welcome feel of the saddle gun under his leg. He had left the

Fifty with the skinners, so he wouldn't have to handle its heavy bulk on the ride. Now he wished he had it.

"Most of those horses looked like good ones," he commented. "Mighty good for Indians."

Shad Blankenship reined up, intently studying something ahead, then nodding as he satisfied himself that it was nothing to be alarmed about. "Comanches are good horsemen. Besides, they probably stole most of these from the Texans. Every fall, before winter sets in, they raid the settlements. Generally strike in the full of the moon. Comanche moon, they call it down there.

"Steal horses, women, children, anything else that ain't nailed down. What they don't steal, they kill or burn up. Then they hit it off back up to this country and winter on these plains. Ain't nobody ever reached them up here. The only ones know the trail are the Comanchero traders out of New Mexico. They're strictly contraband. They come out and trade for the stock the Indians have stole. That's where the Comanches get the guns and powder and other white-man stuff you see them with nowadays."

Sticking with the brush, they followed the trail six or seven miles along the edge of a draw that led eventually to another creek, much like the one on which the hide hunters had been camping.

They caught the drift of wood smoke before they saw the village.

"Yonder it is," Shad whispered finally, "on that flat aside the creek."

Jameson slipped out of the saddle and lifted the

binoculars from the saddlebag again. He could feel his hair stiffen as he looked down on the tall buffalo-hide lodges, forty or fifty of them, strung out up and down the creek. It seemed to be a new camp, for the grass was not trampled out yet. Smoke curled upward from the smoke flaps, which were opened downwind. Indians hurried up and down through camp like so many ants, cutting the fresh buffalo meat into strips for drying, spitting huge chunks of it to be roasted immediately. It was mostly a woman's job from here on. The warriors who had done the killing now lolled around in camp, some of them washing themselves in the cold water of the creek.

Dogs fought up and down the camp site, struggling over fallen scraps of meat. Some of the children threw rocks at them. One pair of scrapping dogs felled a squaw, causing her to drop a huge chunk of red meat in the sand. Grabbing a stick, she chased the tail-tucking dogs all the way down to the creek while loafing men made fun of her.

Elsewhere, other women were working on the fresh hides, pegging them out, scraping them religiously clean to they could be tanned later with a mixture of liver and brains. Watching, Jameson lost much of the tension that had drawn taut within him.

Suddenly he saw something that didn't belong, something that made him draw his breath in sharply and lower the binoculars, lifting them again as if he didn't believe it.

Then he handed them to Shad. "Take a look," he said, his voice unsteady. "See if that's really a white woman there, scraping a hide."

Shad took the glasses, searching among the lodges. Then he stopped. His red-bearded jaw dropped. 'By George, I do believe it is. There I see a squaw kickin' at her. She's a captive, right enough."

His binoculars back, Jameson studied the woman. He couldn't tell much about her. She wore deerskin clothing, old and greasy, evidently the castoffs from some squaw. He couldn't make out her face or guess her age. He could tell only that she was slender, even thin, that her light-colored hair reached far down below her shoulders.

He saw a brave come up behind her, look around quickly, then grab her long hair. He jerked her head back and with his other hand made the sign of scalping her. Then he gave her a rough shove forward.

A curse came up under Jameson's breath. His hands gripped the glasses so hard that they hurt. He saw another Indian walk up angrily and berate the brave. This man, Jameson thought, was probably the chief of the band—at least a leader of higher rank than the warrior. Even so, the warrior paid him scant attention. He turned insolently and strode off, leaving the leader staring after him.

For a moment then, the leader studied the white woman, who had gone back to scraping the green hide. She didn't look at him. The chief turned and walked away in a dejected attitude.

Jameson lowered the glasses. "Shad, I don't know how we're going to do it. But we're going to get her out of there!"

9

"YOU'RE CRAZY, Jameson. It's not worth the risk."

Ransom King paced angrily back and forth before the campfire, his eyes jabbing at Jameson. "Do you really think you could get that woman out of here?"

Jameson stood motionless, his questioning gaze drifting from King to the other men standing around in the edge of firelight. He was still half stunned with surprise. He had never expected this opposition from King. Now he wondered how many more felt as King did.

"We've got to try."

"You think the Comanches will just hand her over to you? Have you any idea how it could be done?"

"I've got a notion how we might do it."

"*Might* do it!" King's voice was heavy with sarcasm. "*Might*. Even by the tone of your voice you admit how slim the chance is. You're crazy,

Jameson, you're about to jeopardize everything we've come down here for. Use a little judgment, man."

A stir of anger worked at Gage Jameson. It colored his voice. "King, I thought you'd be the first one to say 'Let's go.' Now I don't know what to think. I know it's not cowardice."

"Of course it's not cowardice. It's common horse-sense. I've got an investment here, a big investment, and a chance of a big return. So have you. Do you think I want to throw it away, and maybe die too, on a ten-to-one chance of rescuing some woman you saw through a pair of field glasses? How do we know who she is, or what she is? She may have been there so long she doesn't even *want* out. Ever think about that? For all we know, she might be some dance-hall floozie like Rose."

"Even if she was," Jameson said, "I'd do it."

"Then you're an even bigger fool."

Stiffly they faced each other over the campfire. The men watched them silently, staying back in the edge of darkness. Jameson couldn't tell how the sentiment went.

"Listen, Jameson," King argued, "Blankenship says they probably took her on a raid in the Texas settlements. A Texan. They were almighty independent a few years ago. If those Rebels want her back, I say let them come up here and take her themselves. I spent four years fighting them. I wouldn't risk what I've got here for a freightercar load of them."

"She's a white woman, King. You can talk all

night, but you can't alter that."

King rocked back and forth on his heels, chewing his lip, his eyebrows drawn down half over his eyes.

"A woman. Just because it's a woman we're supposed to give up everything and go. It always did make me tired, listening to high-flown talk about the sanctity of womanhood. They put women up on a pedestal like some brass god, when all the time that's all they are—just brass. I've known a lot of them, Jameson. Even married one once. They're just animals like the rest of us. No better and perhaps a lot worse."

Jameson attempted to answer to that. Even in his anger he could understand King. Only two things meant much to this brash hide hunter—excitement and money. Money most of all.

King made one last attempt. His voice was level now, persuasive instead of bludgeoning. "Look at the percentages, Jameson. Chances are heavy you won't even come out alive. But *if* you do, stop and consider. We've had good hunting here. There are still plenty of buffalo. Indians haven't bothered us to speak of. This new camp probably doesn't even know about us. We can move twenty or thirty miles and they never will know.

"But what happens if you raid that camp? Then we've got to move, fast and far. We may have to go so far to get out of their reach that we'll run out of buffalo. Those wagons are half empty yet. It would mean ruination, Jameson. Ruination."

But to Jameson there was no choice. There hadn't been one since the moment he had seen the woman in that Comanche camp.

He turned away from King, turned to the other men.

"I'm not telling any man he's got to go. There's no use lying to you, it's going to be dangerous. But I'm asking for volunteers."

The camp was silent and still, except for the cold night breeze moving through, flickering the camp-fire. Jameson searched the faces, red in its glow. Shad Blankenship stepped up beside him.

Reb Pruitt solemnly took off his sack apron, laid it on the chuck-box lid, and walked to Jameson's side.

Then came the lank skinner Messick. But there it stopped. Vainly Jameson looked to the men for more help. They stood there, staring at the fire or at the ground or off into darkness, not meeting his eyes. And then he realized.

It was King. King had hired them for him. Even yet their allegiance was to King, not to Jameson. Disappointment settled within him.

Four against the Comanche camp.

A shadow raised up from out in the darkness somewhere. Ludlow, his beard black as the night, walked up, folding a knife blade against his leg. He shoved the knife into his pocket and tossed a whittling stick into the blaze. He gave the other men a lingering look of contempt and stood beside Reb Pruitt.

Five now. And five was all it was going to be.

Knowing that, Jameson said to them, "I won't hold you to it. You know five is mighty slim."

They didn't move.

Reb Pruitt said, "She's a Texas woman, Jameson. I'll go if I have to go by myself."

Jameson didn't say it, but the thought ran through his mind: No wonder it took us four years.

Then King restlessly dug his toe into the ground. "Oh, the devil," he said, "no use being so dramatic about it. We'll all go."

Looking around quickly in surprise, Jameson saw him nod.

"It's still a crazy fool idea," King said grudgingly, "and it'll probably get us all killed. But I knew all the time we'd have to go, if we couldn't discourage you. We can't afford to lose you, Jameson. This expedition would sink like a rock in the river."

Jameson smiled and shook King's hand. "Thanks, King. I knew you weren't afraid."

"Afraid? The only think I'm afraid of is that someday I may get as stupid as you are. Call me when you're ready. I'm going to catch me some sleep."

For Jameson there was no rest. He put the men to breaking camp, loading the wagons. When they got back—*if* they got back—these wagons had to be ready to roll.

At last he lay down in his blankets, but sleep wasn't in him. He turned restlessly awhile before he gave it up. He looked wonderingly at Shad Blankenship, rolled up and snoring. Shad could sleep through a cannonade.

Jameson got to his feet and walked to the chuck wagon. He dipped water from a bucket and into the coffeepot. He poured a little fresh coffee among the old grounds and set it all on the coals, punching them up for extra heat.

He heard Reb Pruitt's voice behind him. "That's *my* job."

He turned and tried to smile. That wasn't in him, either. "Guess neither one of us can sleep."

They sat there watching the pot, wondering if it ever would come to a boil. He felt a deep need for talk, for something to take his mind off whatever was coming.

"What part of Texas are you from, Reb?"

"South Texas. The brush country."

"Fought in the war, did you?"

Pruitt nodded. "If you could call it fightin'. I got there late. Seemed like mostly all we could do was retreat and listen to the officers tell us we was just backin' up for a fresh run at the Yanks. We was always out of powder or lead or something to eat. Seemed like all we had left was guts, and they ain't worth much when your stomach's empty."

"It wasn't much fun for us either, Reb."

Pruitt poked restlessly at the fire. "I reckon not."

Sitting there watching Pruitt, Jameson felt a strong liking growing in him for this lean, hungry-looking little cowboy cook. There was more to the man than had earlier met his eye.

"It's none of my business," Jameson said, "and you can say so if you want to. But they tell me you got in trouble down there and can't go back. Something serious?"

Pruitt shrugged. "I shot a yellow-leg cavalry lieutenant with a sawed-off shotgun."

"Kill him?"

"No, I wasn't tryin' to. But where I hit him, it put him in the infantry for a good spell."

Only a pale rind of moon lighted their way as they moved along. But Jameson knew the direction. He kept his horse unerringly on it, moving at a jog trot across the silver tableland. Ransom King rode silently beside him, keeping his thoughts to himself.

Behind them came the men, all except a few they had left to guard the wagons and have them ready to move. Poker-playing Blair Farley had elected to stay, perhaps taking to heart what Jameson had said about someone shooting him during the thick of action to keep from having to pay a gambling debt.

There hadn't been enough saddles to go around, or horses either. Several rode mules bareback. As they strung out of camp, Jameson counted fourteen men.

Angling across the flat prairie, they finally struck the other creek. Jameson reined up, studying it in the darkness. He looked at the Dipper, judging the amount of time he still had before daylight. The early-morning chill had him stiff, his back aching a little from the cramped way the cold had made him ride.

"Pass the word back," he whispered. "It's not far now. Nobody talks. Nobody smokes. One wrong move and there'll never be another."

He touched spurs lightly to the horse, easing him down into the bitter-cold creek and across.

His heart quickened as he heard the other mounts splashing over behind him. Crisp air like this could carry sound a long way.

Up the other side, he kept riding, getting off some distance from the water. He remembered the line of timber and brush that had lain behind the village, indicating a draw that fed water into the creek in time of rain. This draw, he figured, would give them cover. He looked back again and saw the men bunched up close behind him, guns in their hands, ready.

Stars in the east had begun to pale when they moved their horses and mules up into the brush behind the village. Jameson caught the grease-smoke smell that always betrayed an Indian camp. The wind had stilled now in this pre-dawn darkness, but the chill was sharp enough to set a man to trembling.

He dismounted to let his horse blow, and the others followed his example. They walked the horses, leading them to cool them down gradually.

As the sky lightened, he could pick out the lodges one by one, their conical shapes rising up against the horizon, the poles above the smokeflaps showing clearer in approaching dawn. He was looking at the village from the opposite side now, and he no longer could be sure exactly where he had seen the white woman. He waited, and studied, and finally he thought he knew which lodge it would be. The question was, did she sleep there, or was it merely one where they made her work?

He could see no movement in the camp as yet. Part of it, at least, would be because of the buffalo the Indians had taken yesterday. They would have gorged themselves last night, eaten all they could stuff in, and then they would have fallen into a drugged sleep.

Scattered throughout the length of the village he saw horses hobbled or staked, twenty-five or thirty head. But most of the horses—a couple of hundred—were in a loosely-held herd down past the lower end of camp, scattered over several acres of flat, grassy ground along the creek. Way out to one edge he saw an Indian horse herder sitting sleepily on the ground, holding the leather rein of a mount that stood droop-headed over him.

Jameson had had little experience with Comanches, but he knew within reason that an Indian on the war trail would never be far from his horse. Even sleeping, he would have the mount staked or tied close at hand. Stealing horses from a war party was well-nigh an impossibility, unless you were another Indian.

But now the Comanches were on their own ground, seemingly inviolate here on their inpregnable Llano Estacado, easing down to the long monotony of winter life. And like white soldiers when they thought they were safe, they had let down their guard.

"We've got to have that horse herd," Jameson whispered to Shad.

Shad chewed heavily on his tobacco, frowning, his pale eyes leisurely working from one end of the camp to the other, not missing a horse track or a buffalo bone.

"Then let's just take it," he said casually.

He pointed his red-bearded chin. "That second

lodge from the end yonder—ain't it the one where we seen her?''

"Yep." Jameson felt more secure in his judgment now, for he had picked the same one.

"Reckon she's still there?" Shad asked.

Jameson shook his head. "I hope so. It's the best bet we've got."

"The minute they see what we're after, they'll kill her."

Jameson's hand was tight on the saddle gun. "I know it. So we've got to get her before they see what we're really up to."

He lifted his chin, studying the sky. Light enough now, he thought.

"Shad, I want you to take King and most of the men and run off that horse herd. Make a lot of noise. Push it straight across the creek, and be in a hurry. The Comanches will be boiling after you like a swarm of hornets."

Shad smiled a little at the anticipation of action. ''And how do you figure on amusing yourself in the meantime?''

"I'll take Pruitt and Ludlow and Messick. While you draw the warriors off on that end, we'll get busy down here. Later on we'll meet you somewhere across the creek, on the way back to camp."

He paused, then added, "If we're lucky."

Shad and the other riders moved away slowly, keeping under cover of the brush. Jameson held his breath until his lungs ached, listening for a giveaway noise like a horse stumbling or snorting in this knife-sharp morning air. It seemed to him that the strike of hoofs was gunshot-loud, but he knew that was imagination. Any minute he expected the camp dogs to sound the alarm.

He worried most about those men riding bareback. An Indian could give you a whale of a fight bareback, but these were white men used to saddles. Some weren't used to riding at all. They would have a hard time just staying on, if the going got rough. Their guns wouldn't be much help.

For a time then, Shad's men were out of sight as the brush swallowed them up. There was not even the muffled sound of hoofs. Jameson turned to the remaining three men. "Better check your guns again. One miss-lick now and we're dead."

A dog began to bark, somewhere down toward the horse herd. Another dog picked it up, and another and another. In a few seconds the alarm had racketed back into camp, every dog there adding to it his own excited yelp. Holding his breath again, Jameson peered through the brush and saw the horse guard straighten, looking around.

He thought desperately. Now's the time, Shad, if you're ever going to do it!

And Shad did it. A sudden rattle of guns exploded toward the horse herd. Snapping unexpectedly out of sleep, the horses jumped one way and the other in excitement. The riders thundered down on them, firing guns, and they stampeded.

For a moment it looked as if they would plunge straight into the Indian camp. But someone intercepted them, headed them off. Then they were running for the creek.

Jameson watched the horse guard raise his rifle. Half a dozen bullets ripped the Comanche apart.

Pandemonium struck the camp. Warriors burst out of the lodges, rifles and bows in hand. Some shouted in confusion. Some took wild shots at the raiders who swept away their horse herd. Those who had horses tied or hobbled nearby ran to them. Even some of these horses jerked free in panic and stampeded through the camp, galloping after the herd. While the warriors ran after the raiders in helpless fury, squaws and children hurried out of the lodges to see what was taking place.

Jameson lifted his binoculars and watched that second lodge. Then he saw her. She stepped through the flap and stood watching the dusty, pounding scene of wild confusion.

"There she is," Jameson said quietly to Pruitt, shoving the binoculars back into his saddlebag. "You ready to get that Texas woman out of there?"

Pruitt nodded gravely. They swung onto their horses. Jameson jabbed with his spurs. The mount burst forward in a lope, out of the brush, racing swiftly toward the woman. She was about two hundred yards away. Or was it two miles?

Rifle steady in his hand, Jameson spoke tensely under his breath and realized suddenly that he was praying. He kept spurring. He could hear the clatter of hoofs behind him and knew the other three were right with him.

The hadn't been spotted yet. Jameson couldn't see a warrior anywhere who might oppose them. They had all run toward the other end of camp. But a man couldn't dismiss those squaws. They could fight like so many wounded panthers if they needed to.

The captive white woman saw them. For the space of two or three seconds she stood numb, not believing. Then she broke into a run toward them.

Squaws saw them now. They waved their hands excitedly, most of them turning to flee, shooing the children before them. But one, with a knife in her hand, started running after the white woman. The woman saw her and tried to run faster. But the squaw was fleet-footed and gained rapidly. Jameson raised his rifle but realized he couldn't fire accurately at the speed he was riding. He might hit the wrong woman. His heart clutched in dismay. He knew he couldn't reach her before the squaw did.

Then, just as the squaw closed the gap and raised the knife, a gunshot roared behind Jameson. The squaw stumbled, rolled in the grass and lay still.

Reb Pruitt had slid his horse to a sudden halt, thrown his rifle to his shoulder and fired. It was a perfect shot.

Heart racing, Jameson pulled to a stop, kicked his left foot free and reached down for the woman. She put her foot in the empty stirrup. He gave her a quick boost up behind him. Then, as her arms clasped tightly about him, he spurred the horse again.

Arrows began to whisper past them as some of the closer warriors saw what was happening. Even a couple of squaws had bows and were stringing arrows, letting them fly at a speed Jameson would not have believed if he hadn't seen it. He kept spurring. They were out of effective range already.

If an arrow struck them now it would be by sheer accident. A few rifles sounded behind them, and Jameson could hear the deadly sing of bullets.

Jameson took one quick glance over his shoulder. He could see the tense, shock-pale face of the woman—a young woman she was—and her long blonde hair streaming in the wind. He could see his three riders close behind him, not one appearing to have been hit. It had gone off so quickly that it had been over before the Indians could act by anything other than reflex.

Now Jameson put his horse into the creek, splashed across, and spurred out on the other side again. They broke through the tangle of brush, then were out on the open prairie, running free.

10

To HIS RIGHT Jameson could see the horse herd still running, necks outstretched, legs reaching to gather in the miles, the dust rising up from the dry grass. He reined that way, staying in a hard lope. He couldn't see behind him well, but he knew there was certain to be immediate pursuit on any horses the Indians had managed to keep in camp.

Through the patchy brush he could see Comanches on horseback, pushing across the creek in a splash of water that flashed a spangled reflection from the rising sun. He couldn't count them, didn't try.

"You all right?" he asked the woman behind him, speaking to her for the first time. Her answer, in a voice strained almost to breaking, was barely audible. "I think so."

He caught the wood-smoke smell of Indian and knew it was from her frayed old deerskin clothes. He could feel her body against him, trembling, but it might well have been because of the cold. She had no coat against the chill of the morning. Even the sleeves were gone from the old squaw dress she wore. They had splashed a lot of icy water moving across the creek.

He had caught only a fragmentary glimpse of her face, but now he could see her hands, clasped tightly to the front of his coat. They were young hands—red, raw and bruised—but they were strong hands, hands that knew work.

Shad Blankenship edged out from the horse herd and angled his mount toward them at a run. Relief washed over his rough old face as he saw the woman and noted that none of Jameson's group was hurt.

"We got company comin', young'un," he shouted against the wind and the hammering of hoofs.

Jameson looked back over his shoulder at the line of Indians. Fifteen or eighteen of them. They were making a gain, for the hide hunters were hard pressed to keep the horse herd moving on.

He got another look at the woman too. He saw deep blue eyes etched with pain, a face haggard from hardship and taut with the remnants of fear. A mouth with lips drawn in tight, a chin firm and strong, indicating the fortitude to face up to what might come.

Ahead Jameson saw a buffalo wallow, not deep but good enough for at least some protection. He pointed to it, and Shad saw, nodding. Shad waved his hat. The men with the horse herd began pulling toward him, letting the Indians' horses run on. Pushing hard, they converged on the buffalo wallow. The Comanches were coming in, making it a tight race.

Jameson slid to a stop in the wallow and let the woman swing to the ground. The place was a depression, possibly thirty or forty feet across, where the louse- and fly-ridden buffalo came to wallow in the dust for relief from the constant itching.

Jameson motioned the woman to lie down against the bank for protection. The other hide men rode in and jumped from their horses and mules. Urgent though the situation was, not a man failed to stop long enough to glance at the white woman. Even Ransom King.

"Hold onto those mounts," Jameson yelled. "This is no time to be set afoot."

Kneeling, lying prone, some of them standing, they waited. Bridle reins were tight in their hands or looped over their arms, the rifle barrels bristling at the edge of the buffalo wallow.

The Indians closed in, shrieking and yelling.

"Hold your fire till they get close," Jameson said loudly. "Then get the horses, that's the main thing. Don't let a horse get away."

He raised his saddle gun, lined the sights on the Indian in the lead. This man, he realized suddenly, was the chief he had watched through the glasses yesterday. He waited, his breath held until a slow fire kindled in his lungs. Then he squeezed the trigger. The rifles on either side of him roared. Some of the hunters' horses and mules broke loose in terror and plunged away.

He saw the chief jerk back, clutch desperately at

the horse's mane, then tumble off to struggle out his last breath on the ground. Other men's bullets tore into the charging line. Horses stumbled and went down. Indians rolled in the grass. Some jumped to their feet, some lay cramped and still where they had landed. Men and horses screamed in pain. The murderous gunfire went on. Jameson fired again and again, each shot bringing down a horse.

In seconds every Indian horse was hit. The vicious fire had riddled the Comanche line like a scythe whispering through wet grass. Few of the Indians had had time to loose an arrow or fire a shot. Now many were dead or wounded, and the rest were afoot, their fallen horses thrashing.

The surviving ones tried to return fire, bellied down in the cover of grass or behind the fallen mounts. In the wallow a mule screamed and went down kicking.

But the hunters poured out a fearful hail of lead. They didn't have time to let themselves get pinned down here, Jameson knew, and he figured the others realized it, too. Given time, the Comanches would have reinforcements afoot from the camp.

Half the hunters had lost their mounts, either from their jerking away and running or from the Indians' fire.

One man lay on his face in the wallow. Jameson felt of him and shook his head. He had skinned his last buffalo.

"Mount up double," he ordered. "We've got to clear out of here."

He and Shad and a couple of others kept up fire

while the rest mounted. Then they swung up, too, and they moved out in a run.

This time the woman was in the saddle and Jameson was behind, protecting her. The few remaining Comanches fired after them. Jameson heard a man cry out. Reb Pruitt drooped in the saddle, an arrow in his arm. Thinking the Texan might fall, Jameson pulled in beside him and caught him, holding him in the saddle.

"I'll make it," the little cook said through gritted teeth. "Nobody ever had to hold me on a horse yet."

They rode a mile. Then, knowing there could be no pursuit, Jameson reined in and stopped Pruitt's horse. He slipped off and helped the cook down. The woman swung to the ground.

"Bleedin' like a stuck hog," Pruitt breathed painfully, as if ashamed of himself for getting hit.

"Through the flesh part of the arm," Jameson said. "Arrowhead went through clean."

Shad Blankenship took one man to each mount and went after those horses and mules that had run away.

Jameson took out his knife and cut the arrowhead from the shaft as carefully as he could. It was a steel one, he noted in anger. Something from the Comanchero trade.

"Can you help me hold him?" he asked the woman. Tight-lipped but looking as if she knew what she was about, she put her arm around Pruitt's shoulder and held tight.

Jameson gripped the shaft and said, "This is going to hurt, Reb. Grit your teeth and cuss or say anything you want to.''

Pruitt nodded, white-faced. ''Just get on with it.''

Jameson jerked. The shaft came out clean. Pruitt's head rocked back, his eyes shut, his jaw clamped hard. Slowly he expelled his breath and opened his eyes. They were moist with pain. But he managed a semblance of a grin at Jameson, and at the woman.

''Wasn't so bad. First time I've had a woman's arms around me in I don't . . . know . . . when.''

He slumped back, unconscious.

''Shock,'' Jameson said. ''We'd better stop the bleeding.''

With her help he pulled off Pruitt's coat and rolled up the sleeve. The other men crowded around to watch. Blood flowed slowly, sticky and warm. Jameson searched his hip pocket for a handkerchief. He frowned at it. Not clean, but the best he had. He bound it tightly around Pruitt's arm. The cook was beginning to stir again. The woman held his head, keeping him as still as possible.

''That'll hold it,'' Jameson said at last. ''We can do better when we get him to camp.''

He really looked at the woman for the first time now, admiration warm in him at the calm way she had helped him with Pruitt.

''You've got a steady nerve,'' he said.

''The Comanches taught me that,'' she replied.

It was hard to guess at her age. She might have been anywhere between twenty and thirty. Captivity had ground harsh lines into what must have been a pretty face, or close to it. The fear was gone from her eyes now, but a lingering of pain was still there. Her lips were dry and cracked from the sun and wind. Her long blonde hair was wind-tangled but freshly washed, and it appeared to have been combed out not too long ago. The thought came to Jameson that it was lucky she hadn't been killed way back yonder instead of being kept captive. Many an Indian would give his right arm to own a scalp like that one, to keep it brushed down so it would glisten in the firelight at night as he bragged to other warriors about the many scalps hanging from the point end of his lance.

She was shivering again. The morning air was still cold. Jameson took off his coat and held it out to her. "Here. Put this on."

She took it hesitantly. "What about you?"

"I've got a heap to do. Being busy will keep me warm."

The coat was twice too big for her, but he could see the relief in her eyes at the warmth of it.

"We don't even know your name yet," he said.

"Westerman. Celia Westerman. And yours?"

"Gage Jameson. Where did the Comanches capture you?"

"Down on the San Saba, in September."

September. Two months and more. She had been through it, all right.

"A great many women would have died before now," he said.

She nodded gravely. "That might have been the easiest way," she replied.

Shad Blankenship and some of the others had brought back the runaway mounts and had rounded up the Indian horse herd again. Jameson looked it over. He picked a few of the best-looking to replace the animals that had been killed in the buffalo wallow.

"Brands on most of them," Shad observed. "Been stole, almost every hoof in there."

Ransom King's eyes glowed as he looked at them. "How many would you say there are, Blankenship?"

"Two hundred, a few more or less."

"They'll fetch a price in Dodge," King commented enthusiastically, the dollars shining in his eyes.

Gage Jameson frowned and checked his saddle gun. "We're not taking them to Dodge. We're shooting them."

He thought King was going to burst, the way anger made his neck veins stand out. "You're crazy, Jameson! Think what they'd be worth in Dodge!"

Jameson said flatly, "We've got no right to sell them. They're stolen horses."

"What owner is ever going to get a chance to claim them? They were lost when the Comanches got their hands on them. It's salvage now, Jameson, same as a sea captain salvaging a wreck."

"I don't know anything about salvage laws. But I know these are stolen horses. We've got no right to sell them."

King's voice went almost shrill in anger. Here was money, easy money, untainted by blood and grease and the smell of dead buffalo. And it was slipping from his grasp.

"Then what right have you to shoot them?"

"Just this: afoot a Comanche isn't much. Let him get on horseback and you're in trouble. They'd steal these horses back from us, King. We've got all we can do to keep them from taking what stock we already have. Take this many more and we'd likely lose them all, our own stuff too. Then we'd be in it for sure. As long as these horses are alive, they're a millstone around our necks."

King declared, "I don't care what you say, Jameson. If you're going to shoot them, I'll claim them. They're mine."

Short of patience, Jameson flared. "Take them, then. Take your wagons, too. Cut out for Dodge the quickest way you can."

That stopped King. He stood stiffly, hands clenched in fury. But he was whipped and he knew it. His wagons were not yet half full of hides. He had come after hides, not horses. Alone with his small crew of men, he wouldn't stand a chance of getting to Dodge with those horses. They would be stampeded before he could travel thirty miles, perhaps his own stock with them.

He shrugged, anger still splotched red in his face. But he was helpless to alter the situation. He forced a smile that wouldn't stay.

"Shoot them, then. You're the wagon master."

He started to walk away, then stopped to look at Celia Westerman. His narrowed eyes swept over her, head to foot. A lingering of malice was in his voice. "What about *her,* Jameson? Now that you've got her, what'll you do with her? She's a little like the horses, isn't she? A millstone around your neck?"

Jameson glanced at Celia Westerman, then quickly looked away as he saw a sudden tightening in her face.

King had hit him squarely. He had been so busy trying to free her that he had given no thought to what he would do afterward. The hide camp was no place for a woman. Yet what could he do about her?

Hating the horse-killing job and now confronted with another problem, he spoke to Shad a little curtly, and instantly regretted it. "What're we standing here for? Let's get this job done and move out."

With his saddle gun and a pocketful of extra cartridges, he walked out toward the horses. He flinched, his stomach coiling in revulsion at what he had to do. Then he raised the rifle.

11

JAMESON was glad to be on the move again, to get away from this place with its gagging stench of gunpowder and blood, the screams of the dying horses still in his ears. Someday men would come upon this gaunt stretch of bleaching bones and wonder what great massacre had occurred there.

Celia Westerman rode beside him, knowing what put the bleakness in his face. "There's no point in worrying yourself about it."

He nodded grimly. "I know. But I've never had a job I hated so much. A man gets a feeling for horses, depending on them the way I have. Shooting them is almost like shooting people."

She was silent awhile, studying him as the group rode westward, driving the few animals they had chosen to keep.

"I don't know how to start saying thank you. I don't know any words half strong enough."

He eased a little then. It had been many weeks

since he had heard woman-talk. He liked the way she spoke, slowly, deliberately, not quite a drawl like Reb Pruitt's, but slow anyway.

He said, "I know what you mean. I've been in the same kind of fix myself."

"But why did you do it? You didn't even know who I was. It was a terrific risk to take for a stranger."

"You were a woman, a white woman. That's why we did it."

"That seems mighty little reason, looking back on it."

Jameson said, "Several times in my life I've been in a tough spot, something I couldn't get out of by myself. Somebody always came along. Most often it was a stranger, sombody I never saw before or ever saw again. Seems like we go through life owing gratitude to strangers. The only way we can ever repay them is to help some other stranger. It all evens up, in the long pull."

Then he said, "To your family, I suppose it'll be as if you'd come back from the dead. Married?"

She shook her head. "Not married."

"Father? Mother?"

"I still have my father and a couple of brothers. I lost one in the war."

She studied him gravely. "I haven't figured out yet what you men are. You're not Rangers. You're not Comancheros. What are you?"

"Buffalo hunters. We're down from Kansas."

"From Kansas." He caught the disappointment before she managed to cover it up, and he knew what she was thinking. She had hoped they were Texans, that they could take her home.

"We'll find a way to get you home," he promised.

Some of the pain went out of her deep blue eyes, and a brightness came to them, shining warmly. "Home." She spoke the word softly, caressing it.

He watched her, and Ransom King's words came back to him. A millstone around his neck. He felt a nudge of anger at King for saying it, yet he realized that in a sense it was true. He had Celia Westerman now. But what could he do with her?

The circled wagons looked deserted. Gage Jameson reined up to study them, for caution was second nature to him. He motioned Celia Westerman to hand him the saddle gun from the scabbard beneath her leg. She did, and he signaled her to pull back. The other riders approached warily too, rifles ready.

Then there was movement at the wagons. The men who had been left on guard stepped out into sight, holding guns. They stared curiously at Celia Westerman.

"We couldn't tell at first," fat Blair Farley spoke with nervousness. "You might of been Injuns."

The stock was all inside the circle. Camp was broken. The wagons were loaded. The only thing still to be done was to catch up the mules and hitch them to the wagons. But Jameson looked at the men around and saw the fatigue heavy in their faces from the long night ride, the hard action, the strain and the fear. Hunger gnawed at him, and he knew it must be the same with the others.

"We could do with a strong meal before we get moving," he said. He looked at Reb Pruitt, stretched out now in the shade of the chuck wagon. Reb hadn't lost much blood. Most of what ailed him was shock. Two or three days, he'd be doing a one-handed cooking job and talking his head off. Right now, he wasn't in much shape to talk or to help.

"Shad," Jameson spoke, "you're a good hand with a coffeepot and a Dutch oven. Let's see what we can fix to eat."

Celia Westerman had been kneeling beside Pruitt. Now she stood up and came to the chuck box. "Here," she said, "I'll help."

Jameson said dubiously, "You've been through a lot. Don't you think you ought to rest?"

She shook her head. "No, I can't afford to sit still right now. If I ever did . . ." She held out her raw hands for him to see. They trembled a little. "I might go to pieces. I've got to keep busy till I can steady down."

Jameson nodded. "I guess so. But cooking for a bunch like this isn't exactly a woman's job."

"I grew up on a cattle ranch. Lots of times I've cooked for a big crew. Just help me find what I need."

Jameson built up the fire again while Shad Blankenship put fresh coffee in the pot.

"Ignorant hide skinners," Shad grumbled, they throwed out the old grounds. Can't make good drinkin' coffee without the old grounds."

Jameson climbed into the wagon and cut fresh hump meat. Watching Celia Westerman handle the Dutch ovens and the big pots, he knew she hadn't been bluffing. She had done all this before.

Presently the coffee was boiling and fresh meat was frying deep in bubbling grease inside a lidless Dutch oven over the fire. Reb Pruitt always kept biscuit dough made up for days ahead. Celia Westerman broke the dough into biscuit-sized wads and put it in ovens, setting them on live coals. Jameson heaped more coals on the lids when she finished.

There wasn't much to do now but wait. Jameson sat on his heels close by the chuck wagon and watched Celia Westerman. Occasionally his eyes drifted to the eastern horizon, but no anxiety was in them. Having left these Comanches afoot, he had no fear of immediate pursuit. Still, he knew it was high time to clear out of this part of the country. They wouldn't be afoot forever.

Something was worrying Celia Westerman. She carried it a long while, then looked at Jameson. "I keep thinking about that man who died back there in the buffalo wallow. He died for me, Mr. Jameson."

"It was a risk we all took. We all knew it before we started."

"But *he* died, and I was saved. I can't help thinking about it. What was his name?"

"Andregg. Milt Andregg."

"Milt Andregg." She tried the name. "What kind of man was he?"

Jameson shrugged. "A good buffalo skinner. Beyond that, I don't know much." He knew a little, but it was pointless to bring it up. The man was dead now. The manner of his death compensated for whatever he might have been or done before.

"Did he have a family?"

"None that I knew of."

"I hate to think of him lying back there unburied. You know what the Indians will do."

"You couldn't help that. None of us could."

"No, I guess not. But someday I'm going to put up a marker for him, in a Christian cemetery. It'll tell his name, and what he did. Then he'll always be remembered. As long as a man is remembered, he's not really dead, is he? I mean, as long as he lives in somebody's mind. . ."

"I don't know. I've never thought about that kind of thing very much."

She lowered her head. "I have, lately. I've had lots of time to."

Jameson could see a little of the pain come back into her eyes as she remembered.

"You want to talk about it?" he asked. "Maybe it would help."

She nodded. "Maybe." Her face seemed to grow older as she thought back on it, and the harsh memories crowded into her mind. She hesitated a little, then she started to tell it.

"Times haven't been easy, these last few years in Texas. The carpetbag government took our ranch away from us. I'd been to school, so I got a job teaching. It was a small log building at the edge of town. Hadn't been any Comanche trouble there in a long time. We never even thought about it any more. One afternoon a storm came up just as I was letting out school. Most of the kids ran for it. But there were a little boy and girl—brother and sister—who had to ride five miles home. It wasn't more than a good thunderhead. I figured an hour or so and it would be over. So I told them to stay.

"They came in the rain, the Comanches did. They were in the schoolhouse before we saw them. We didn't even have a gun there. One of them, his name was Kills His Enemies, took a liking to my hair. He had a hatchet in his hand and was about to kill me when the leader came in. I found out later his name was Buffalo Finder. He looked me over, and he made Kills His Enemies turn me loose. Later, Buffalo Finder told me he'd wanted me for a wife. They took us out and put us on horses.

"They had made quite a foray. It was a big raiding party, no squaws or children along. They had perhaps four hundred horses that they had stolen from the ranches. They knew white men were after them, so they pushed hard.

"Some of them spoke a little Spanish, and so could I. It was rough on all of us, but especially on that poor little boy. He was sickly. He couldn't keep up. The first day in the rain was too much for him. He got sicker and sicker and was holding back the bunch. They wouldn't even let me help him.

"Kills His Enemies kept beating him with a mesquite limb. The third day, two of the warriors took the boy out in plain sight of us and pitched him into the air. And when he came down, Kills His Enemies was waiting with his lance. . . ."

Celia Westerman closed her eyes. A tear squeezed out and found its way down her cheek.

"He's a devil," she said, her voice tight, a deep hatred rising in her face. "A devil out of hell."

"Somewhere up on the cap rock we joined the squaws and children they had left behind. Then we came on up here to the high plains to a deep canyon, bigger than anything I've ever seen. A creek runs down the middle of it, and in places the walls go straight up for hundreds of feet. We camped there a little while. Mexican traders—Comancheros—came in and traded for about half of the stolen horses.

"One of them tried to trade for me. He said he wanted to return me to my own people, but that wasn't it at all. I could see it in his eyes. He offered a lot of trade goods, but Buffalo Finder wouldn't give me up. Then after him came an older man, named Felix Alvarez, and he was a kind one. He took pity on us, the girl and me. He said he had lost a daughter about my age. He traded for the girl. She's on her way home by now. He offered everything he had to get me free. But the chief still wanted me for wife. And Kills His Enemies still hoped to get my hair. The old man stayed until he knew it was getting dangerous for him. And when he left, there were tears in his eyes.

"The day they left, I stole a knife. I walked down to the creek, and I tried to kill myself. But I couldn't do it, Mr. Jameson. I was either too strong or too weak, I don't know which. Life is hard to turn loose of, even when there's little left in it. I tried to hope Felix Alvarez might still find a way to rescue me. But I guess I knew he couldn't. It would have been suicide to try, and the little girl would have died, too.

"The chief started trying to get me to consent to be his wife. He didn't have to do it that way. He could have forced me. But he wanted it to be of my own will, I guess. I held off, hoping. And all the time, I knew I would die if I didn't. He had other wives. The number-one wife was jealous. If anyone tells you a Comanche woman can't make life miserable for her husband, he just doesn't know.

"And Kills His Enemies was working on him, too, trying to trade for me. A few days ago we moved here to set up a permanent winter camp. I knew the time was getting short. Either I had to submit to Buffalo Finder or let my hair hang from Kills His Enemies' lance."

Celia Westerman looked darkly at the ground.

"I've always been taught that death is better than dishonor. But it's easier to say it than it is to face the decision and die. I should be ashamed to admit it, but it's the way it was. I had just about made up my mind when you came. I didn't want to die.

"You killed Buffalo Finder this morning. I saw him fall. Kills His Enemies will take over now. He won't stay afoot long. He'll get horses and he'll be after you if you're anywhere on these plains. That's the way he is. He's not human."

Jameson looked into the cook fire a long tim, admiring her strength, trying to make up his mind. "How far would it be to a Texas settlement?"

She shook her head. "I don't know. Perhaps a couple of hundred miles. If you're thinking about trying to take me, don't. No white man has ever done it, so far as I know. Only the Indians know the way."

"Couldn't you find the trail back, the way you came?"

"We made it too fast, and we made a lot of it at night. You have to know the waterholes. A quarter-mile miss on some of them and you're lost. I couldn't be sure I could find them again."

Grimly Jameson said, "Then the only way out is Kansas. We can take you to Dodge. You catch a train to one of the trail towns, and then you can get one of the Texas cow outfits to carry you home with them when they go back."

She looked over the wagons, and her shrewd blue eyes quickly sized up the situation. "It's a long way to Kansas too. And those wagons aren't more than half loaded with hides. If you take me now, you'll hurt yourself, won't you?"

He would ruin himself, he knew. But he wouldn't tell her that. "We've got to get you home."

She shook her head again. "Not at that price, Mr. Jameson. It's been a long time. I can wait a little longer."

"A hide camp is no place for a woman."

He looked around at the men. As he had expected, most of them were staring at Celia Westerun. A woman in a hide camp could cause as much trouble as a woman at sea, if luck took that kind of a turn.

"I know what you're thinking," she said. "But there won't be any trouble. I won't let there be any trouble."

Judgment told him to say no. But he couldn't

keep from looking at his hide wagons, only half loaded.

"You sure you want it this way?" he asked her, wanting her to say yes but afraid that decision would not be the right one.

"You'll hardly even know I'm here," she told him. Then she stood up and walked to the fire, to lift the lids off the ovens of brown bread and to take up the buffalo steaks.

A crinkle came to the corners of Jameson's eyes. There she was wrong. Never for a minute would he forget she was here.

12

FIVE DAYS they angled westward, working generally up the Canadian, and a little to the south of it. They crossed several creeks and streams of varying sizes. Along most of them Jameson found ample sign of buffalo. The land took on a sandier texture as the wagons moved westward. There was more of bunch grass in places. But mostly it was still the short, thick turf of buffalo and mesquite grass, strong feed that kept his horses and mules fat on a minimum ration of corn.

Five days, and he thought they had gone far enough.

Reb Pruitt was cooking again now, with help. He remained pale, his left arm tightly bound. But his feet were as active as ever, and his mouth too.

Because of Pruitt's bad arm, Jameson had suggested getting one of the other men to drive the chuck wagon for him.

"I can do it," Celia Westerman offered. "I've handled wagons almost ever since I was big enough to climb up on one by myself."

So Reb Pruitt rode beside Celia Westerman on the chuck wagon seat, his eyes taking on the glow of a pet dog's. He would have thrown the coffeepot at anyone who had offered to take over Celia Westerman's driving job.

"Handles that wagon better than I could," Pruitt told Jameson in admiration, watching her pull it into place. "I always could make a hand with a bronc, but I never was no great shakes with a team. That there's a woman, Jameson."

The little cook frowned. "Just one thing worries me, and that's them squaw clothes. They ain't fitten for a white woman. We got to do somethin'."

Jameson agreed but didn't know what they could do about it. "I don't know what she could make a dress out of. All we've got is a wagon sheet, and that wouldn't be of much account."

Pruitt reached into the chuck wagon bed and fetched down a canvas bag. "I got some extra clothes with me. Little as I am, it might be some of my stuff would fit her."

Jameson smiled. "I don't know that shirt and pants would be much more proper than what she's wearing now."

"At least they didn't come from no heathen." Pruitt gave second thought to that and grinned a little. "No, heathen *Comanche,* anyway."

Celia Westerman's presence in camp was making some difference. Reb Pruitt wasn't the only one who had taken up shaving almost every day. Even old Shad took to washing the tobacco out of his beard and combing his rusty hair regularly until one day he studied himself awhile in the cracked mirror he used, then pulled a gray hair out of his head and scowled. He grunted something about a chuckle-headed old fool and lapsed back into his accustomed habits.

The new hunting grounds were as good as those they had been forced to vacate, far to the east. Jameson was still bringing down twenty to thirty buffalo at a stand, most days. One time, when there were enough in one bunch for him and Shad to shoot together, they brought down fifty-three head without having to move more than three hundred yards.

November was well along, and he expected a howling blizzard to come streaking down across the plains almost any day. When it finally came, it wasn't so bad. Only one day was it so cold that they had to stay in camp, and there were only a few flurries of dry snow that never even settled on the ground, blowing about like so much powder. Soon the weather was warm and the hunting was good again. Even better than before.

In spite of this, Jameson found himself getting restless, wanting to go somewhere else, do something else, though he didn't know what it was.

He sat at a distance, watching the skinners work through the buffalo he had shot. First, with their straight-bladed ripping knives they would rip down the belly, starting at the throat and working all the way back to the tail. Then they circled the legs below the knee, slitting down to the belly. They cut the hide up to the ears, leaving the thick mat of curly black hair that grew on the huge head.

Taking their curved skinning knives, they then

began to slice beneath the hide until the neck and legs were skinned free and the hide had been worked at least halfway down from belly to backbone. They used pritch sticks with a nail in one end to prop the carcass, feet up, so they could work down the tallowy sides.

This much done by knife, they rolled up a big flap of hide at the neck and tied it to a rope, with a pair of mules hitched on at the rump end of the buffalo. They shouted and flipped the reins, forcing the mules to peel the hide backward off the carcass.

Shad Blankenship rode up and dismounted, stretching himself, then squatting down beside Jameson. "What's the matter, Gage? You got a nervous look."

"It's just those skinners. Seems to me they're getting almighty slow lately."

Blankenship watched them a little. "Ain't nothin' slow about that. It's just you. You got the itch to get back to camp, and it ain't for supper, either. That Texas girl has got you goin' in circles, young'un, the same way she has Reb Pruitt."

Jameson felt the color rise in his face. Shad was striking mighty close to home.

Jameson had felt it coming on for several days. He would look at himself in Shad's mirror and snort the way Shad had. Thirty-five years old, already getting a fair sprinkling of gray in his hair. What was he doing, thinking about Celia Westerman?

But he liked to watch her, liked to listen to that gentle, slow way she had of talking.

As the days went by, the harsh lines in her face began to fade. She seemed to get younger. She moved with a new buoyancy, her captivity drifting into the past like a nightmare after the awakening. Occasionally now she even sang a little as she worked around the wagon, helping Pruitt cook as he had never cooked before.

She still wasn't really pretty, if a man wanted to look at her with a critical eye. But she had a way of making a man think she was.

To Shad Blankenship, Jameson said, "I was worried about her. I was afraid she might bring trouble in camp. It looks like I was wrong."

Shad said dryly, "We ain't in Dodge yet. They're all watching her, don't ever think they ain't. And Ransom King—you take a look at his eyes sometime when he's got them on her. That feller has more on his mind than buffalo hides, I'm tellin' you."

The days went by, and the hides piled up. Dried hides had to be taken off the ground to make room for green ones coming in. Jameson watched with satisfaction as the handlers pitched these flint hides onto a wagon. After awhile it was loaded, lashed down securely with thick strings cut from a green hide.

Another load finished.

"We haven't got far to go now, Shad," he said. "We've got to move camp in a day or two. I think we'd just as well work over the Canadian, start drifting north a little."

Shad nodded without enthusiasm. Jameson could see what was working on him. Shad didn't relish going back to the settlements. It would be the same old story with him, soon as he got there. He knew it, and he was fighting it.

Jameson had something to worry about too. Usually, with the prospect of an early return to town and the payoff, a hide crew got a new spring in its step, got to feeling jolly. But not this one. A tension was building, something hard to trace, hard to put his finger on. More than once he had to step in and stop a fight.

Even Reb Pruitt commented on it.

"Maybe it's the Indians," the cook volunteered. "You don't see any, but the air's got an Indian smell to it, someway. They're around. You can feel it."

To make it worse, Blair Farley had gotten brave and gone back to playing poker. And he was winning. A majority of the men in camp had fallen victim to his skillful fingers to one degree or another. Some already had lost more than they could hope to earn out of the whole expedition. Trencher was one of these. He stalked around the camp like an angry bull, brooding over his losses. Everyone stayed out of his way.

One morning in the first flush of dawn Jameson sat up straight in his tent. He had heard someone shout. He listened a moment and heard it again. Pulling on his boots, he hurried out. He saw several men moving toward the edge of camp.

Someone was calling, "Get Jameson!"

He quickened his step, and the men moved aside for him.

On the ground, a hundred feet past the stock corral, a fat man lay sprawled in his own blood. It was Blair Farley.

A skinner named Darcy Crosson stood by the body, excitement flushing his face. "Injuns," he said breathlessly. "Blair didn't come wake me for guard duty like he was supposed to. I found him thisaway."

Jameson knelt beside the dead man. Farley had been killed with a knife, a cruel ripping job that had laid his stomach open. And he had been scalped. It was rough, crude work that made Jameson's belly tighten, just looking at it.

"Bloody Comanches," somebody breathed in anger.

"Maybe," Jameson said. "And maybe it wasn't Comanches at all."

The men looked sharply at him. He said, "There's hardly a man here who didn't owe him money, lots of money. Now nobody owes him anything."

He could see the idea strike them like a hot iron. They looked furtively at one another, each wondering if the man standing next to him had been the one who had wielded the knife.

Shad Blankenship came up. Jameson asked him, "He always kept those IOU's in his pocket, didn't he?"

Shad nodded. Jameson knelt and went through Blair Farley's pockets one at a time. They were empty, all of them.

He left all the pockets turned wrong side out, letting the men see them, letting them answer the question for themselves.

Someone went for a shovel, and someone else brought out a tarpaulin to cover the body. No one seemed to mourn Farley. Lately he hadn't had a friend in camp.

Shad Blankenship stood with eyes narrowed, watching Trencher lean idly against a wagon.

"Gage," he said, "you got any ideas?"

Jameson nodded. "One or two."

Blankenship's lips drew thin. "I reckon they're the same as mine."

One morning Celia Westerman walked out of her tent and moved toward Jameson.

"Do you know what tomorrow is, Gage?"

He shook his head. "Thursday, I think. Or maybe Friday. I haven't been keeping much track."

"It's Thursday. Thanksgiving. I wish we could have something special to fix for the men tomorrow. They've been brooding a lot the past few days. Maybe a good Thanksgiving meal would cheer them up."

Jameson brightened a little. How many Thanksgivings had he gone through and not even given them a thought?

"You might have something there. Yesterday I flushed a bunch of wild turkeys in a chinaberry thicket up the creek."

Next morning he dug out a shotgun that he had shoved away among the gear in one of the wagons. Filling his pockets with shotgun shells, he motioned Shad Blankenship to him.

"Shad, how about you doing the buffalo shooting this morning?"

Shad looked him up and down, eyes dwelling on the shotgun.

"I'm going to get a few turkeys for Celia," he explained. "She thinks they might go over good with the crew for Thanksgiving."

Shad's eyes took on a glow of humor. "Now you're gettin' some sense. I only wish that when I'd been younger there'd been somebody for me to shoot turkeys for."

Jameson saddled his bay, sliding the saddle gun into the scabbard. The shotgun was all right for turkeys, but that saddle gun would always be handy in case something else showed up over the hill.

Celia Westerman walked out to the corral, wearing one of Pruitt's coats buttoned up to the neck against the winter wind. "Could you use some help? I'd like to go."

He hesitated, liking the thought of her company but a little skeptical just the same. "Always a chance of Indians."

"You'd be there, Gage," she smiled. "I really would like to go. I'd like to get out of camp a little while, just for a change."

He relented, knowing how monotonous it had been for her. "I can get another shotgun, if you want it."

"All right. I used to be a fairly decent shot."

He wasn't surprised. He had quit being surprised at the things Celia Westerman could do.

They rode out together, past Ransom King's wagons and hide grounds.

King stood and stared at them as they went by. He nodded at Jameson. Then he tipped his hat to Celia, and his eyes followed her. There was a trace of hunger in them. Time King was getting back to Rose Tremaine, Jameson thought.

Celia looked behind her once, but she didn't speak until they were well away from camp.

"I'm not sure I like your friend King," she said.

"King's all right, Jameson replied. "He just takes a little getting used to. He's up on a cloud one day and deep in darkness the next. He's wild, he's brash, and maybe a little selfish. But I guess it's selfishness that has made people stick with this country. Nobody would put up with it all, unless he thought he could get something out of it."

Celia frowned. "I know this—that if it had been up to him, I never would have been rescued from that Indian camp."

That blabbermouth Pruitt, Jameson thought with sudden impatience. "Who told you a thing like that?"

"Nobody. I just know it, that's all. I know that if it hadn't been for you, Gage, I'd still be there. Or I'd be dead. I'll always be in your debt."

Jameson found himself pulling closer to her, wanting to touch her but not doing it.

"You don't owe me anything, Celia. It's me that owes you. You don't know what it's been worth, having you in camp. In a way I'm going to hate to see you go home."

She nodded, and her blue eyes met his. "I know. In a way I'm going to hate to go. Sometimes I find myself wishing I could stay here. This is a good country, Gage. It'll be a good country to live in, someday."

They looked at each other until Jameson felt a warmth rising in his face, and a strong compulsion to reach across and pull her to him, to kiss her with all the hunger that was in him.

Suddenly he brought himself out of it, self-anger rising in him. Darn it, this isn't some dance-hall girl like King's Rose. What am I thinking of?

He rode silently awhile, trying to put his mind on other things. But she was too close to him.

"You said you aren't married," he said. "Are you promised to anybody?"

She looked at the ground, her eyes absently following her shadow. "Not exactly. There's a man there—we grew up together. We've talked about it some."

Jameson drew up within himself. Well, he thought, that puts an end to it. Now maybe you can get your mind back on the buffalo.

13

REB PRUITT put water on to boil as soon as he saw them coming, turkeys flung across their saddles. Jameson had no desire to get into the work of cleaning the birds. But he stood and watched as Pruitt and the girl did it. The Texas cook handled the job with ease. Jameson finally asked him:

"How did you ever come to be a camp cook, anyway?"

Pruitt looked up, laughter in his eyes. "Well now, I used to have to ride a lot of rank broncs, back there on that ranch where I worked. One day they fetched me one I couldn't ride, and they had to leave me at the wagon to heal up. I got to watching that fat, lazy cook. Come to find out he was makin' fifteen dollars a month more than I was, and he didn't have no saddle rubbing a callus on his rump, either. So right then I knowed I'd missed my callin'."

Shad came in and unsaddled. He'd had a good stand. Now he sat down, back to a wagon wheel, gun kit in hand. He stripped down his big buffalo rifle, swabbing its barrel clean and wiping a thin trace of oil on it before putting it back together.

Jameson brought the empty cartridge cases he had been soaking in vinegar to get all the burned powder out. Now he set the cases up on end and poured black Dupont powder out of a can into a bowl. He started filling the shells with powder, stopping half an inch from the top. He tamped it down with the rammer, put the wad in, and spilled a little more powder atop the wad. He wrapped a piece of paper around the base of the bullet, then forced it into the shell, clamping it down tight.

"Get your turkeys?" Shad asked.

Jameson nodded.

Shad said, "Great country for game, ain't it? Man wouldn't never starve here, he had powder and lead, and a little salt. He could live fine, the way we done a long time ago."

That far-off look was in Shad's eyes. He was back into times long past, savoring some elusive fragment of fond memory. "It's like the rest of the country used to be before they come and ruined it." He considered that and added, "Before *we* ruined it."

"I know what you mean, Shad," Jameson replied. "It's been that way with me. I get a feeling about this country, a feeling that maybe this is what I've been looking for all my life. You ever look out across it at sundown, Shad? Sundown's the time to look at a place, if you want to see the beauty in it. I get a feeling I don't ever want to leave. I want to stay here, and I want the country to stay just like it is."

Shad grunted, some bitter taste coming in his mouth. He spat and rubbed a greasy sleeve across his red beard.

"But it won't. Three, four years, the buffalo'll all be gone, the way they was from the Republican and the Arkansas. What would there be to stay for? How would you make a livin'?"

"I don't know for sure, Shad. I've thought about cattle. I guess Reb Pruitt put it in my head, always talking about the Texas cow business. This would be a fine cow country, Shad, as good for cattle as it is for buffalo."

"You'd have to get the Comanches off first, and they might not see it just your way."

"When the buffalo are gone, Shad, there won't be any more trouble with the Comanches."

Shad nodded. "But you've never had any experience with cattle, other than maybe popping a whip over a bull team. Takes more than bulls to run a cow ranch, I expect."

Jameson smiled. "A man can learn. *We* could learn, Shad, you and me together. The frontier is going. This would give us something we could both tie to."

Shad Blankenship's wrinkled old face held the beginning of a smile, and his pale eyes were looking far off again, far back into memory. Then, slowly, the smile faded. The memory was gone. The present was here again with its jarring reality. The present, and the future.

"Won't work for me, Gage. I'm too old to change over. The only hope I got is that when my time comes I can die out here someplace and be buried where I can listen to the wind blow and the wolves howl, instead of in town where all I can hear is a piano clinkin' and somebody bellyachin' about the price of beans.''

He pointed his finger at Jameson, jabbed it at him.

''But *you* can make the change, Gage. Make it before it's too late. Get you those cows, and grab onto some of this land. And get you a wife, young'un. I never had one, and that's where I made a mistake. Life gets pointless for a man when he ain't got a home, ain't got a woman of his own. One of them dance-hall gals is all right for a young man still sowing his oats. But comes a day he needs to settle. You've come to that day, Gage. You watch or you'll pass it up, and then it's too late. You need a good woman, like that Celia Westerman. If I was you, I wouldn't let her get away.''

Shad was right, Jameson admitted to himself. He wanted Celia Westerman. He needed her. But it seemed she already had gotten away, even before he met her.

The whole crew was waiting when at last the turkey was done. The sun was going down. The stock had been fed, and all the work had been finished. Nothing was left but to sit down and enjoy the Thanksgiving meal.

The anticipation of it was having the effect Jameson had hoped. The tension had eased.

Even the burly Trencher showed a semblance of a smile as he roughly shouldered his way into the line, digging a fork into one of the turkeys and knifing off a huge section of it.

But something went wrong. The first man to fill his plate shoved a big bite of turkey into his mouth and started to chew, grinning. The grin suddenly left him. His mouth twisted. He spat it all out, choking. Seeing that, another man judiciously tested a small piece of the turkey on the tip of his tongue. His face stretched awry in dismay.

Not seeing them, Trencher bit off a big chunk. He spat turkey for six feet, coughing. He looked up then, a flash of rage in his eyes. He flung the plate to the ground and stalked toward Reb Pruitt.

"You miserable, dried-up Johhny Reb, you're tryin' to poison us all!"

Pruitt stared at him, uncomprehending, until Trencher made a grab. He stepped aside quickly. But Trencher kept coming. He pinned Pruitt to the chuck wagon, swung his big fist and knocked the cook to his knees. He grabbed the little Texan by the shoulder and jerked him erect again. He slammed him against the wheel.

Jameson took long strides across to the wagon. He grabbed Trencher's arm and held it. "Stop it, Trencher!"

Trencher struggled with him, trying to free himself. "I'll kill the little whelp!" he grunted.

Finally, seeing he couldn't pull free, he whirled on Jameson.

"All right, Jameson," he breathed, "I been wantin' to do this for a long time." His eyes glowed with a wild fever of rage. He rushed at Jameson, his arms reaching forward from his heavy body. Jameson did not try to dodge. Instead, he lowered his head and drove straight into Trencher's hard belly. He made Trencher overreach, while his own fists pounded into Trencher's ribs. The big man grunted at the shock, and he reeled a step or two sideways. Jameson kept pushing, pressing this initial advantage, driving at Trencher's belly and ribs.

But the surprise lasted only a moment; then Trencher had his wits back. He plowed in now, his rage driving him on. He was apparently oblivious to the worst punishment Jameson was able to give him. He fought only to win, his heavy feet grinding down on Jameson's toes, his knee trying at Jameson's groin, his fingers grasping and twisting Jameson's ears. Pain rocketed through Jameson, pain and desperation. He knew Trencher would kill him if he could.

Somehow he managed to bring up his knee, hard and quick. His heavy boot smashed against Trencher's shin, taking the hide as it drove downward. Jameson saw an opening and arched a fist into Trencher's ear. The big man cried out and turned away from him. Jameson's fist slammed into Trencher's kidney, once, then again. Trencher doubled over. Jameson jerked Trencher's head up and hit him hard in the throat. Trencher fell heavily to the ground and lay there gasping.

Jameson took a couple of steps backward, heaving for breath. The chuck wagon was behind him. He moved to it and leaned on it for support, his chest rising and falling rapidly as the breath came back to him. He wiped a dusty coat sleeve across his forehead, and it came away wet.

For a moment his eyes were off Trencher. He didn't see where Trencher got the gun. Suddenly there it was, in the man's trembling hands, and Trencher was standing spread-legged, grinning with his lips while his eyes crackled with hatred.

"Now, Jameson," Trencher breathed heavily, and the barrel tilted upward.

Jameson could only stand there, his back to the chuck wagon, staring helplessly at the six-shooter. His mouth went dry. All he could think of was, Where did he get that gun?

He sensed a sudden movement beside him. Trencher jerked aside, but not in time. A heavy iron pot hook from Pruitt's chuck box slammed into the man's head. Trencher fell heavily, the gun dropping from his fingers. Before he could grab it, someone else had it. Messick, the skinner. Jameson looked around and saw Pruitt still bent forward, the way he had been when he let the pot hook fly away, singing.

"Thanks, Reb," Jameson whispered.

As suddenly as it had begun, it was over. Ransom King helped Trencher to his knees. "I'm sorry about this, Gage," he said. "Trencher has a bottle hidden away somewhere, and he's been working on it. I'll get him sobered up. It won't happen again."

Jameson tried to speak, but his throat was leather-dry, and no sound came out. He watched narrow-eyed as King and one of Jameson's own men helped Trencher stagger away.

Angrily Trencher jerked free of the men who were holding him. He turned half around, his hate-filled eyes on Jameson.

"I'll get you, Jameson. Your time is about run out. I'll get you and don't you forget it!"

King took hold of the man and roughly yanked him away. "You're drunk, Trencher. Come on."

Celia Westerman hurried to Jameson. Her fingers anxiously explored the cuts and bruises on his face. "I'll take care of those," she said.

He waved his hand. "Never mind. I'm all right."

But she went anyway to the chuck box, hunting for antiseptic. The rest of the crew melted away, chewing on bread, sipping coffee, but leaving the turkey alone. Pruitt stared at it, puzzled.

"I can't figure it out. I know it wasn't nothin' we done. But that meat's so bitter it makes you sick."

It struck Jameson then, as Celia painted his wounds with iodoform. The chinaberries. He hadn't thought of it before. The turkeys had been feeding on chinaberries. That had tainted the meat.

"Dandy Thanksgivin'," Pruitt said disconsolately. "Nothing much here to be thankful about."

Jameson slowly shook his head. "One thing, Reb. We can be thankful we've got those wagons about loaded. I think it's high time we headed for Dodge."

14

"RAININ' WAY YONDER," Shad Blankenship said, watching the heavy clouds scurry across the morning sky. "It would rain here too, if a man was to look at them clouds a little cross-eyed."

Jameson could smell the promise of rain in the sharp wind searching across the prairie. Riding beside Shad, holding the Big Fifty in his lap, he frowned at the skies. "Maybe. Been hoping it would hold off a little. Three or four more days and we'd have all the hides we can pack."

"We got plenty now," Shad said. "She starts in to rainin', we better settle for what we got and move out."

Shad spat, and his big black dog jumped aside. Shad let his pale eyes lift to the horizon. "Something else too, and that's that Injun, Kills His Enemies. I'd just as soon not have to mess with him. But there's Injuns around, Gage. I can feel them in the back of my neck."

When Jameson smiled, Shad said quickly,

"Don't laugh. Dodge them as many years as I have and you get so you don't have to see them any more. You can smell them, like a hound dog."

Jameson looked back toward the two wagons that trailed them, slackening his pace when he saw that they were getting some distance behind. Like Shad, he was getting that uneasy feeling, wondering each day if it might not be smarter to pack up and string the wagons north than to ride out for another day's bag of green hides.

They didn't have to ride far to find buffalo, for a big herd had drifted in along the creek where they were camped. The animals grazed in scattered bunches up and down it for miles. They were almost black now with the thick coat of winter hair that made them look bigger than they had a few weeks ago. These winter hides would bring more money. With that heavy hair they could be turned into robes instead of being cut up for leather.

It was this that had kept Jameson here, the robe hides and the ease of the kill. Had the buffalo been hard to find, he would have started north a week ago.

"Well, Shad," Jameson said, "let's split up and get this over with as soon as we . . ."

He broke off, for Shad had stiffened. Jameson turned quickly and saw what Shad saw—Indians.

Ten warriors swept down the crest of a hill toward them, whooping and yelling as they came. Ten warriors against two men, with the wagons still behind.

"We can't get back to the wagons, Shad!" Jameson exclaimed. "They'll cut us off."

Desperately he began to look for a hillock, a

buffalo wallow, anything for cover. But there was nothing.

Shad stepped out of the saddle and dropped prone to the ground. He began to dig in his pocket. "Good a time as any to see if that man was right about these squallers," he said. He was as casual as if he were about to try a new gun on the buffalo.

Jameson had almost forgotten about those bullets Shad had bored the holes in. Now, dropping down beside Shad and ramming one of his own cartridges into the breech, he remembered.

Shad raised the rifle and fired. The bullet screamed as it sped through the air, the bored hole catching the wind. Shad put another one in and fired again.

"Squall like a banshee, don't they?" Shad said.

The Indians hauled up short, and Shad put a third one over their heads.

"I only got two left," Shad complained. "If they don't work, I'm gonna have to tell that feller he's an awful liar."

He fired the fourth one. Now the Indians began to pull back, gesturing excitedly. Shad balefully eyed the last bullet, then slipped it into the breech. It was even louder than the rest, one of the weirdest sounds Jameson had ever heard. It made the hair stand on his neck.

It did the job. The Indians wheeled their horses and took out across the hill again. Jameson lowered his own rifle, still unfired.

Shad grinned and spat tobacco juice out across the grass. "Superstitious lot, Injuns are. Come up against them with somethin' they ain't seen or heard before, and they don't hardly know how to take it. Come to think of it, somebody shot one of them things at me, I wouldn't know how to take it either.''

They stood up, catching their horses.

Jameson looked at the hill over which the Indians had come and gone. And he made a decision.

''I think we've got all the hides we'd better try for. We're heading north, Shad, while we still can.''

Swinging back into the saddle, Shad nodded in agreement. ''Now, young'un, you're talkin' sense.''

They rode quickly back to the two wagons, not knowing if the Indians had been frightened enough to keep away, or if they might come back over that hill at any minute.

The men at the wagons had pulled up together and jumped to the ground, rifles ready. They still stood there as Jameson and Shad rode up.

The tall, thin skinner Messick solemnly shook his head. ''We thought sure you was goners, both of you. And we wasn't even sure about us.''His eyes went to Shad. ''What in the name of heaven was that you shot at them? Not even a Comanche can make a sound worse than that.''

Shad explained the squallers. ''Worked this time. But they'll probably figure it out. Next time they won't be so easy fooled.''

Jameson said, ''Turn the wagons around and head for camp. There won't be a next time if we can help it.''

They had not ridden three minutes before they heard other gunfire, farther away. Ransom King's. You could always tell by the sound of the guns who was doing the shooting. No two of these buffalo rifles made quite the same report.

Suddenly Jameson straightened, his ear turned toward the sound. The first tremor of alarm moved through him. There were more guns than there ought to be, and the firing was getting faster. That wasn't the way you shot buffalo. Jameson glanced at the other men and saw that they were listening too.

"They've hit King," Jameson said. "Let's roll."

Messick and the other driver flipped their reins. The mules lunged forward, jerking roughly against the traces, bouncing the wagons. Jameson spurred into a lope and took the lead. Shad Blankenship fell in just behind him. Jameson leaned forward in the saddle, listening to the crackle of guns.

He looked back and saw the wagons trailing behind him, moving as fast as they could without bouncing the wheels off.

A mile. A mile and a half. The shooting was close now. They topped out over a ridge and there the battle was, below them. King and Trencher and two skinners were barricaded behind an upturned wagon. Around them lay four dead mules and King's sorrel horse.

A dose of our own medicine, Jameson thought.

Around and around the men fifteen or eighteen Comanches circled, whooping, yelling, letting arrows fly into the flimsy barricade. Three or four Indians and as many horses lay fallen on the prairie. And inside the barricade Jameson saw a man lying still, on his stomach.

He signaled the wagons to pull up, for he saw no

practical way to get them down off the steep ridge in time to be any help.

"We'll do a better job shooting from up here anyway," he said to Shad. The skinners piled out and came running, bringing their rifles. Jameson signaled one man to hold the horses and mules, the rest to spread out in a line. He bellied down in the grass, put up the rest stick for his Sharps and drew a bead. The first shot sent an Indian horse plunging into a somersault. Beside Jameson, the other men opened fire. Two more horses went down, and Indians fell.

The Comanches hauled up in surprise. While they stood there, trying to locate the source of fire, well-aimed bullets cut down two more. One Indian made a signal, and the others followed him, leaving the battleground in a run. Jameson sighted down the barrel, held his breath and squeezed. The Indian who had signaled pitched to the ground. The others kept riding.

The hide men on the ridge continued rapid fire, and the men behind the barricade were doing the same. Another horse fell. The rider jumped up limping. Two Comanches turned back, leaning down and drumming heels into their horses' sides. Riding on either side of him, they picked him up and carried him off between them, holding him that way until they thought they were out of bullet range.

Presently Jameson stood up, pulling the rest stick out of the ground, wiping the dirt off of it onto his pants leg.

"Looks like it's over, Shad."

"Maybe. And maybe it's just started."

A drop of water struck Jameson's hat brim. He looked up, and another hit him on the cheek. His gaze went to the horizon. He saw that it had faded out into a gray pall of rain.

"Fixin' to get wet," he said. "Let's see what we can do down there."

Without going back for their horses, Jameson and Shad walked down the ridge toward King's upturned wagon. Messick followed behind them, using his rifle to help his balance as his long legs hurriedly worked down the steep slope.

One of King's skinners walked shakily out to meet them, his face gray as an ashbank, hands trembling. "Man alive, but you fellers came just in time. They had us, I'll tell you, they had us."

King stood beside the upturned wagon, rifle in his hand, the sprinkle of rain striking its hot barrel and turning to steam.

"You saved our hash, Jameson," he said levelly.

Jameson shook his head. "That evens us up. You saved mine once, in Dodge."

But Trencher glared angrily, his hatred for Jameson still burning in his eyes. "We was doin' all right," he said sullenly. "We'd have whipped them off without you." He turned sharply and trudged out to look across the field of battle.

Jameson knelt beside the man who lay face down in the grass. One of King's crew. He touched him, then stood up. The man was dead.

Jameson looked at King. "There'll be more dead if we don't haul out of here. I think I've got all the hides I need. How about you?"

King looked up at the horizon over which the

Indians had poured down upon him. "I'm satisfied. Those boys will be back, and I'd just as soon not be here."

The lean Messick was walking around over the battle scene. At length he paused to look down on three Indians who lay still within twenty feet of each other.

Trencher strode that way, taking a skinning knife from his belt.

"I'm gonna count coup this time," he said brutally.

He knelt by the first Indian, cut a crude circle around the top of the head with the sharp knife and roughly took off the scalp. He moved to the second. But this one wasn't dead. When the half-conscious Indian cried out at the fiery touch of the blade, Trencher jerked back as if he had touched something hot. Then he lifted the knife and plunged it into the Indian's throat. He grinned savagely as he brought it up and stabbed down again.

A moment later Trencher was wiping the knife in the grass and dangling three gory specimens of crude butchery, the grin cutting across his broad, bewhiskered face like a knife gash itself.

Messick stood watching him, his back stiff, some of the color drained from his cheeks. When Trencher had gone, Messick glanced toward Jameson and beckoned him with his sharp chin.

"What does that remind you of, Gage?"

"Blair Farley?"

Messick nodded and said tightly, "Yeah, and even farther back than that. Remember George Hobart, and those two men we found dead with him that last trip out for Miles and Posey?"

Jameson knelt and looked closer at the scalped Indians, remembering how it had been with the white men, wondering if possibly . . .

"Nathan, it couldn't have been . . ."

"But it could. The thought struck me when I saw Blair Farley, but I didn't believe it then. Now I do."

Jameson protested, "He works for Ransom King. How could he have killed Hobart?"

"He doesn't work for King all the time. They tell me sometimes he goes out for himself, when King doesn't need him. Who knows what he does when he's out that way? He's no hunter, Jameson. Man hunter, maybe, but not a buffalo hunter."

"We'd have to be sure."

"That knife he had—I caught a quick look at it. I'd swear it was George Hobart's. George made his own knives, and there never was anybody else ever made one just the same as his."

A chill passed through Jameson. He had to concede that Messick might be right. There was a brutality, a killer instinct about Trencher. Jameson had seen it often enough to know. He'd even been pitted against it.

"We'd still have to have proof before we could do anything."

Messick's eyes were narrowed in cold fury. "I'll get you the proof. I'll get my hands on that knife someway. And if it's George's . . . I'll put it in Trencher's throat, the way I'd do a buffalo."

Jameson closed his eyes, remembering last year when he had helped run down three hide thieves who had murdered a hunter and stolen the hides he had worked months to get. They had gone so far as to scalp the victim, trying to shift the blame onto Indians. But another hunter had stumbled upon the scene and run for help.

Jameson would never forget how they had hanged the thieves one at a time, out on the tree-less prairie. They had used the upended tongue of the stolen wagon. The last two had watched ashen-faced and trembling as the first one had choked and slowly died.

And later, when it was all over, somebody had scalped all three of them.

Messick said, "I'll get that knife. Then we'll see what we do."

The rain was falling steadily as they hurriedly broke camp. They took up the half-green hides from the drying grounds and loaded them on the last empty wagons that had been used to haul each day's bag in from the killing grounds. At the first sign of rain Reb Pruitt had stretched a wagon sheet over the hoops of the chuck wagon to keep the remaining supplies and bedding dry. Then he had stretched a tarpaulin out overhead to give the men a place to stand out of the rain while they wolfed down a quick meal.

Gage Jameson stood on the creek bank, watching the angry swirl of mud-brown water. The creek was rising steadily. A couple of hours more and it would be out of banks from the rain which had already fallen farther upstream.

Shad Blankenship pointed his rusty chin toward the chuck wagon. "You better grab you somethin' to eat so we can drag it out of here."

Jameson shook his head. "In a minute. Just

looking at that creek, Shad. Think we could put the wagons over it right now?''

Shad frowned, watching the brown water rush past. ''Maybe, maybe not. Another hour or so and nothin' will get over it.''

''That's what I was thinking. If we could get across it now, it would give us a lot of protection from the Comanches, at least till it went down. And we could get a long way by then, if we kept traveling.''

Shad rubbed his chin. ''It'd sure be some gamble. We might lose every wagon we got.''

''No telling what we'll lose if we have to fight those Comanches. We'll try it with one wagon— *I'll* try it. If it works, fine. If it doesn't . . . ''

He let it drop there. He turned and hurried back to camp. He sought out the wagon with the smallest load of hides on it and called a pair of teamsters.

''Let's hook a team to this wagon, quick.''

He disconnected the trail wagon while they caught up the mules and put the harness on them. This would be the way, one wagon at a time, then come back for the trail wagons. Seeing what he was about to try, the other men gathered to watch anxiously. They all knew what this meant—a chance to avoid a battle.

Jameson shed his coat, his boots and his hat in case he had to swim. He started to climb up to the wagon seat. Celia Westerman caught his arm. Her blue eyes were big with fear.

She said, ''Gage, I . . .'' Her lips went tight, and she choked off the words. ''Gage, be careful.''

He squeezed her hand, then crossed two of her

fingers. "Keep them that way," he said. He climbed to the seat and flipped the reins.

"*Hya-a-a-a-a!*"

The mules jerked against the traces and the wagon lurched forward, the iron rims slipping in the slick mud. Jameson swung the mules around, straightening the wagon before it reached the levelest part of the creek bank. The mules seemed to sense the danger. They began to falter. He took the long whip and lashed far out with it, popping it over the ears of the leaders, yelling as he went.

The leaders plunged into the water. Jameson kept the whip talking, kept the other mules pulling hard. The foamy water lapped up against the wheels of the wagon as they splashed down off the creek bank.

"*Hya-a-a-a-a!* Keep on moving there! *Hya-a-a-a-a!*"

The mules angled with the powerful current. For a moment Jameson's hopes soared high. It looked as if they would make it to the far bank without a hitch.

Then the full force of the water hit the flat side of the wagon. He felt a sickening lurch. He saw panic sweep through the swimming mules. He found himself wishing they were horses. Mules almost always were the most sensible in a tight, but in the water horses had them bested.

The wagon began to tilt, top-heavy with its load of hides. The mules were fighting, plunging up and down. One went under water, came up, then went down again.

He's lost, Jameson thought fearfully. Let him get his ears full of water and he's lost.

He felt the wagon begin to heave over beneath him. He jumped from the seat into the brown foam, his hands tightly clutching the lines. Over the heavy roar he heard the splash as the wagon went over on its side, then over again, the wheels up out of the water. He heard the snap of the tongue.

The wagon was doomed now, and the mules threshed in terror. Another was out of sight, adding its dead weight to drag the rest down. Jameson managed to grab the bridle of one fighting mule and hold while he drew the knife from his belt. He cut at the harness, trying to free the mules from the wagon.

But the heavy pull of the current wrested the harness from his hands, and somehow he lost the knife. He felt himself being pulled away from the wagon, away from the mules.

All was lost now, he knew, hopelessness sweeping through him. The mules, the wagon, the hides—all of it. All he could do now was try to save himself.

He swam desperately, managing to keep his head above water as the raging current carried him on. He fought to return to the bank. He was working nearer. But his mouth was full of the muddy water. He choked, swallowing some of it. His arms were afire with pain, heavy as anvils.

He realized suddenly that he was drowning, that he would never make it to the bank. Swallowing water, his arms giving out, he was done.

But he kept fighting, trying for the bank.

Then he saw someone out there on horseback, rope in hand. The horseman rode into the water, as far as he could without being swept into the current. Going down, Jameson saw the rope swinging. He fought to the surface again, and he felt the rope settle and jerk tight about his shoulders. Instinctively he grabbed it. He felt it burn cruelly into his flesh as he hit the end of it. Then the rope began to pull him against the current. He swung slowly but surely toward the bank. He felt the slick mud underfoot and tried to help himself ashore. But no more strength was left in him.

The rope dragged him onto the bank, out of the water. He stayed there on hands and knees, coughing up muddy water, nausea sending the world reeling about his head. He was conscious of the clean rain beating down on him.

Reb Pruitt jumped from Jameson's bay horse, dropping his end of the rope. He rushed to Jameson's side. He took off his coat and threw it over Jameson's wet shoulders.

"Go on now," he said gently, "bend over there, keep coughin' that water up. You'll be as sick as a horse if you don't."

Jameson kept coughing. Gradually the world stopped spinning and he could see. "How far . . . how far?"

Pruitt shrugged. "Quarter mile, maybe. That's a mighty fast current."

Jameson caught Pruitt's hand. "Thanks, Reb."

The little Texan grinned, recoiling the wet rope. "You're a pretty decent kind of a Yankee, Jameson, and I figure we better hang onto any of that kind we can get. There ain't many."

Men came running afoot, the quarter mile down from camp. Men, and a woman. Celia Westerman rushed to Jameson. Breathless, seeing he was all right, she threw herself into his arms.

Jameson held her tightly, his cheek against hers. The rest of them were staring, and he didn't care. He held her a long time.

"Celia," he said at last, "we've got to go. It didn't work. All we can do now is travel, and travel fast."

15

MOVING THE WAGONS OUT, Jameson tried to ride his horse. But the muddy water he had swallowed made him lean over and heave until at last he was too weak and head-spinning sick to stay in the saddle. So he moved to the seat of the chuck wagon, beside Celia Westerman, and let the cowboy cook ride the horse.

He had changed to dry clothes. Now the cold, steady rain had soaked even those, and he hunched up in a miserable knot, a raw chill penetrating him to the bone.

He looked back often to the long line of heavy-laden hide wagons strung out behind. Their wide rims cut through the brown cured grass and squeezed dirty water up into deep muddy ruts that ribboned out in their wake.

A blind Indian could have followed them, he thought darkly.

Celia Westerman touched his arm. "Look, Gage, yonder."

He glanced up where she pointed. His eyes still burned from the muddy water, but he could see the eight or ten horsemen far off there in the rain, hunched under blankets, watching the wagons.

"We can't get away from them," Celia said. "They'll follow us until they're ready. And then they'll come."

They kept rolling all the rest of the day and well into darkness. Shad Blankenship and Reb Pruitt rode in front, feeling out the low places for soft spots that might bog down the wagons. The rain was letting up some, for which Jameson was thankful. Much more of it and the ground would become so boggy the wagons couldn't move.

Jameson looked often to the right, and usually he saw the Indians there, following along patiently out of range.

Men in the other wagons were watching them, too. Someone said angrily, "Why don't they come on and get it over with?"

"They're just waitin'," came the answer in Nathan Messick's even voice. "Injuns don't like the rain. They'll come down in their own due time."

When they didn't come before dark, Jameson felt some relief. At least they weren't likely to strike before daylight.

Reb Pruitt came up, and Jameson called him. "Let me have the horse awhile, Reb."

Celia Westerman caught Jameson's hand. "Gage, are you sure you can ride?"

"I feel a lot better now. Anyway, this shouldn't take long."

With Shad Blankenship, he rode along the creek

bank, looking for a likely spot for camp, a spot that would help them present a good defense. The rain had stopped, but the creek was still running high.

"You ain't thinkin' about tryin' to cross her again, are you Gage?" Shad asked worriedly.

Jameson shook his head. "No thanks. I already had my bath."

He found what he wanted, a place where the creek bank had caved back far enough from the water itself so that the stock could all be herded down there out of reach of the Comanches.

"Reb," he said as he rode back to the chuck wagon, "I've found a good place where we can line the wagons up in a row right on the edge of the bank. We'll put the horses and mules down below. That'll give us the water at our backs so they can't circle us. Follow me."

The cave-off was perhaps a hundred yards long and the sharp bank about five feet high, a kind of pocket against the creek. Carefully they pulled the wagons up within feet of the edge, angling the tongues outward so the front of one wagon was almost touching the tail gate of the next. As the teams were unharnessed they were turned loose below the bank.

Working in darkness, the men cut timber and threw up a barrier at each end to keep the stock inside. Reb Pruitt built his fire below the bank with wood he had kept dry all day under the wagon sheet. Shivering with cold, their clothes thoroughly soaked, the men filed by to fill their cups with hot coffee, then went back to work. They shoveled wet earth high under the beds of the wagons as protection against bullets and arrows.

Only when the work was finished did they stop to eat. The hot coffee and the buffalo meat brought strength back to Jameson. His head was clear, and he was no longer sick at his stomach. He could almost forget the soggy clothing sticking to his skin, the cold that stiffened him and turned his lips blue.

Ransom King walked over and sat on his heels beside Jameson and Celia Westerman. "What now, Gage?"

"Nothing, just wait. I don't believe we could find a better place to make a stand. No more running. We'll wait here for them."

King looked worriedly back toward the water, which still roared in the darkness. "What if that creek rises some more?"

Jameson's lips drew tight. "Then our bread just turns back to dough."

Waiting, Jameson reloaded all the empty cartridges he had. Ceila Westerman sat beside him, brooding. "Gage," she said finally, "it's all my fault. If it hadn't been for me, you wouldn't be in this."

Gage shook his head. "It's not your fault. You weren't captured by your own choice. You didn't know we were going to try to free you until we'd done it. There wasn't a thing you could have done or changed. Besides, we'd likely have run up against them sooner or later anyway. We knew when we came down here we'd have a fight getting out. So now we have it."

"What do you think of our chances?"

He shrugged. "We've got a good defensive position here. We've got buffalo rifles that can shoot farther and straighter than anything these Comanches have ever seen. We've got powder and lead, and plenty of food and water. Whatever happens, they'll have a run for their money."

The glow from the faraway campfire barely lighted her face. She was looking at Jameson, her eyes soft. Presently she touched his hand.

"Gage," she said, "do you have a girl waiting for you somewhere?"

"No," he replied. "There's never been one."

She leaned to him a little. She said, "I told you once that there was a man back home. . . . I thought there was, Gage. But I know now that there never was enough between us."

She tilted her head upward. "Gage, whatever happens, I want you to know . . . I love you."

His arms went around her. He pulled her to him, and their lips met in the darkness.

Daybreak, and every man was up, peering anxiously out over the earthwork defense they had piled up beneath the wagons.

"Nothin' there," Shad Blankenship said. "Maybe want us to sweat."

"Maybe they think we're going to move again," Jameson commented. "They want to catch us strung out in the open. But we'll fool them on that. We'll wait right here."

Reb Pruitt called out, "Grub's ready. Come and get it!"

The men filed by, and Jameson watched their faces, wondering how well they were going to hold up. In most of the faces he saw a tenseness, but if there was real fear, he failed to detect it.

Suddenly he became aware that someone was missing. Nathan Messick!

He climbed up on the bank and looked over the camp. "Anybody seen Messick?" he called.

Nobody replied. Most began looking around for him. Reb Pruitt had the loudest voice. He called again and again. But Messick was gone.

"Them Comanches," Pruitt muttered angrily. "They must of snuck up here in the night."

Puzzled, Jameson glanced at Trencher. He noticed that Trencher's knife was gone from the scabbard on the man's belt. And he remembered what Messick had said:

"I'll get you the proof. I'll get my hands on that knife someway. And if it's George's, I'll put it in Trencher's throat, the way I'd do a buffalo."

It hadn't been Comanches, Jameson knew. Messick *had* gotten hold of that knife, sometime during the night. But something had gone wrong.

Jameson looked down at the flooded creek, still rolling and foaming. He knew where Nathan Messick was. He choked back the fury that welled up inside him.

When this is over, he promised himself, I'll get you, Trencher. I don't know how, but I'll get you.

After breakfast they sat and waited, an hour, two hours, three. Jameson watched the clouds lose their heavy gray. Slowly they thinned, the glare of sunlight showing in weak spots. By mid-morning there were definite breaks in them. The rain was over. The sun would be out soon, and the mud would begin to dry. The wagons could move faster.

"Here they come!" Shad Blankenship called.

Men scrambled for their places beneath the wagons. Most lay prone on their blankets to keep out of the mud. They had their ammunition lying beside them, ready.

Jameson looked up and caught his breath. The Indians came in a body, riding at a lope. The solid group spread out fanwise, and suddenly the Indians began to yell.

Jameson was held by the deadly magnificence of the sight. Never had he seen its equal, and he knew it was something he was likely never to see again. Shrieking and yelping, the Comanches came rushing across the rain-soaked ground, waving their bows and lances and guns, their heavy bull-neck shields. The bodies of Indians and horses alike were splashed with red and yellow. War bonnets streamed in the wind. The barbarically painted bodies glinted with metal ornaments and charms. In horses' manes and tails there fluttered bright red cloth, plaited to stay.

Jameson felt the hair lift at the back of his neck.

"Get down, Celia," he said. "Stay down."

She shook her head. "I'll help you reload."

"All right, then. But keep low." Then he yelled for the men, "If they get too close, shoot for the horses. Don't let a horse come through."

He flopped down on his blanket then. He rested the barrel of the rifle across a wagon spoke.

The Indians were bearing down on them, two hundred yards away.

"Trying to ride over us the first time," he said. He drew a bead on one of the nearest Indians and fired. The Indian spun half around and fell off the horse, blown open by the heavy bullet of the Big

Fifty. Other rifles roared. Indians tumbled. Horses sprawled, other horses stumbling over them and crashing down.

The buffalo hunters kept up a rapid fire, lacing the Comanche line. Behind them, under the bank, their own horses and mules milled excitedly. When some of the Comanches appeared to be breaking through, the rifle muzzles tipped downward, and the horses rolled. Two Indians who fell near the wagons jumped to their feet and came running, only to be torn apart by bullets before they reached the breastworks. Others turned and fled afoot, some falling under fire, some managing to swing up behind other Indians who had not lost their horses.

The first attack was broken. The Comanches retreated in a ragged line, leaving the plain dotted with fallen horses. Some of these animals threshed and screamed in pain until merciful bullets sought them out.

The Comanches tried to pick up as many of their dead and wounded as they could before they rode away. Jameson counted ten warriors carried off. He could still see six or eight lying in the grass, too close to the wagons for the Indians to recover them.

One fallen Indian raised up on his elbow and began dragging himself away. A rifle cracked, and he fell face down in the mud. Jameson saw Trencher lower his rifle to reload it, grinning.

The Indians rallied far out yonder on the prairie, milling around, arguing. They would be a little while.

Jameson pushed to his feet and slowly made the

rounds to see how the crew had fared.

'Any dead?'' he called

There was no answer to that, and relief lifted a heavy weight from his broad shoulders. "Any wounded?''

From two places came an answer. One of King's skinners held a rag to his shoulder, stopping the flow of blood from a flesh wound. Face a shade pale, the man said, "I've had mosquitoes do worse."

He found the other man kneeling over, pants pulled down, while Reb Pruitt grinned and poured antiseptic into a cloth, daubing it on an angry red streak across a tender part of the man's anatomy.

Reb said, "You Yanks taught me a long time ago that you had to keep more than your head down.''

Jameson asked, "Think you'll be ready to fight again when they come back?''

The skinner nodded darkly. "Just as long as I don't have to sit down."

Jameson walked to Ransom King's place. "How's it going over here?''

King looked up and grinned at him. "Just send us more Indians.''

Trencher lay beside King on a spread-out blanket. He wouldn't look up at Jameson, just kept scowling out over the muddy mound in front of him. Jameson looked down at the empty knife scabbard at the big man's belt. The anger came back to him.

But he had to bide his time now. They needed every man they had, even Trencher. It might be that the Comanches would get Trencher and

Jameson wouldn't have to.

Jameson returned to his own place and found Celia waiting there, rifles loaded and extra cartridges laid out neatly. He touched her hand.

"I still wish you'd get down below the bank," he said.

She shook her head. "I'll stay by you."

He stood beside the wagon and watched the Indians milling far off in the distance. The group began to move forward again.

"Get ready," Jameson called. "They're coming back."

The tactic this time was the same as before. The Comanches fanned out and came riding in a lope again, shrieking and yelling, their line ragged but unwavering. Brown bodies glistened in the sun, war paint shining. Feathers streamed.

This time Jameson did not wait for them to get near. Lying down, he again rested the rifle barrel over the wagon spoke and took careful aim. At four hundred yards his bullet brought a horse down. The other men began to fire. Long before the Indians were near enough to use arrows or their own guns, the hunters' fire had cut another ghastly swath through their lines.

The Comanche attack this time was halfhearted. Two hundred yards from the wagons the Indians began hauling back before the deadly fire of the hunters' long-range guns. Gathering their dead and wounded again, once more they fled the field.

Jameson had been holding his breath until his lungs ached, cold sweat breaking out all over him. Now he stood up again to breathe heavily. Celia Westerman stood with him, leaning her head wearily against his shoulder. Black gunpowder streaked her cheek.

"Think perhaps they're leaving?" she asked him.

He shook his head. "I doubt it. They'll probably try again."

Once more he made the rounds to check casualties. He was pleasantly surprised that there hadn't been any this time. The Comanches had never gotten close enough.

Shad Blankenship took a fresh chew of tobacco and patted his black dog. "They probably don't know what to make of these big buffalo guns. The way you picked that Indian off awhile ago was enough to set them to thinkin'. Turn them back one more time like that and I'd bet we've seen the last of them."

Jameson was grim. "I hope so."

He went back to Celia and sat down beside her. Her presence strengthened him. He poured water down the Big Fifty to cool the barrel and carefully swabbed it out to remove the burned powder.

"Pretty rough," he said to her presently. "Still think you like this country?"

She picked up the ramrod and used it on his saddle gun. Firmly she said, "It won't always be this way. A few years from now people will be moving onto these plains to stay, to ranch and to farm. There won't be any buffalo or any Comanches."

"What about *you*, Celia? Would you come back here, with *me*?"

Her eyes lifted to him and warmed. "I would, Gage."

"I've thought about it a good many times," he said. "A few more hunts and I'll have enough money saved back to go into whatever kind of business I want to. I've thought that as soon as this country opens up, I could bring cattle here. Shad Blankenship with me, and maybe Reb Pruitt too. Reb knows the cattle business. And after what's happened this trip, I'd want Reb with me wherever I went."

He took Celia's hands and held them. "I've spent a lot of time thinking about the place I'd build. Lately it seems like you're always there with me."

She leaned to him, her head against his chest. "I *will* be there, Gage."

Shad Blankenship yelled, "Get set, boys. They're comin' back."

The Indians began to move toward the wagons, slower now, cautiously. Just outside effective rifle range they broke into three groups. One rode north, one south. The other waited.

Shad Blankenship squinted. "What're they up to now?"

Alarm began to tingle in Jameson. "I'm afraid I know. We've got two weak points, Shad, the ends of the line. They're going to outflank us on both sides."

The worry settled deeply into Shad's pale eyes. "And the other bunch will hit us in the middle, just like they been doin'."

"We've got to pull some of the men out of the middle and use them to strengthen the ends," Jameson decided quickly. He walked down the line, singling out men to move.

"Ammunition is no problem right now," Jameson told them loudly. "So use all you need. Start shooting as soon as you see a target. Thin them out as much as you can before they get here. There'll be more than enough of them left to go around."

He found himself sweating, and he rubbed his hand across his face. It left the acrid taste of burned powder from the rifle-cleaning job. Then he thought of something else.

He dug out four cans of gunpowder from below the bank, where he had placed them to keep stray bullets from striking them. Two he handed to Reb Pruitt. "Run those out there a couple of hundred feet and drop them. When the Indians get on top of them, put a bullet in them, blow them up."

Jameson hurried to the other end of the line with the remaining two. He climbed over the bank and ran out into the grass, a can of gunpowder under each arm. He dropped them off thirty feet apart and ran for the wagons. The shrill cries of the Indians came up behind him. He picked up speed, plunging down the steep bank almost on top of the hide handler, Ludlow.

"When they get on those cans of powder, be good and sure you shoot straight," he yelled.

He sprinted back to his own position and dropped down on the blanket, grabbing up the Big Fifty. He started to open the breech.

"It's loaded," Celia said.

The men along the line had already begun to fire. Jameson drew down on the Indians coming into the center of the line and squeezed the trigger. A horse went down, but the Indian line never faltered.

"They're coming on in this time, I think," he told Celia. "They're going to get us or give up."

The flanking Indians were the closest. They moved in a run, shouting, firing what guns they had even before they were within range. Jameson counted thirty or more coming in on the left flank. As many more came on the right.

Choking gun smoke rose over the buffalo hunters, hovering like a dark gray cloud. Horses and Indians went down, but there were more to take their places.

Jameson felt his heart beat quicken. The flank charges were going to overrun the defenses. There were too many of the Indians to stop. They were three hundred yards away now, two hundred. Now arrows began dropping in behind the wagons. Hunters feverishly worked their breechblocks, keeping their rifles blazing.

On Pruitt's side the Comanches were nearly upon the wagons. Suddenly one of the powder cans went up in a fierce blast, hurling half a dozen Indians to the ground, sending their horses rolling in a cloud of black smoke. Other horses near the blast began to jump and pitch, squealing in panic. The second can exploded. For a moment then, that charge was broken. Bucking horses threw their riders and raced away. Indians left afoot made a run for the wagons, but they were easy marks for the rifles. Those still on horseback gathered themselves for another rush.

One Indian slammed his horse into a wagon, jumped onto the stack of hides and dropped down upon a skinner, knife blade flashing. Reb Pruitt swung his rifle barrel up against the Indian and shot him point-blank through the lungs.

Then the Comanches were coming in on the other flank. Heavy rifle fire had thinned them, but many still were mounted. Someone fired too soon at the first of the powder cans. Its blast set a couple of Indian horses to pitching in terror, but it did little to slow the charge. The Indians came streaming in.

Ludlow pushed to his feet to fire at the second can. It went up almost in the middle of a tight group of Indians.

But a handful of Comanches came on. They sent their horses running headlong at the timber barricade. Two came leaping over. Rifle fire caught one horse in mid-leap and he came down dead, falling on his rider and pinning him helpless against the ground. Ludlow lifted his rifle as the second Comanche came over. The Indian's lance caught him, spun him around. He fell, the lance driven through his body. The Indian whirled, raising his bow and whipping an arrow out of the quiver at his back. Bullets cut him down, even as someone grabbed up Ludlow's fallen rifle and brained the trapped Indian with the butt of it.

Jameson was still firing at the Indians who charged headlong into the middle of the wagon line. They were close now, what was left of them, making a last desperate attempt to overrun the hide men. Bullets ripped into the beds of the wagons, buried themselves in the hides. They puffed up dust and mud from the earthen breastworks. Behind him Jameson twice heard men cry out and knew that this time the casualties were running high.

Heart in his throat, he saw that the Indians were going to overrun the line. He fired so rapidly the gun barrel was red-hot in his hands.

"Get down!" he shouted desperately at Celia. "They're coming in!"

A Comanche tried to jump his horse between two wagons. The animal wedged. Jameson whirled and shot the Indian off the struggling mount's back.

Another Indian came over a load of hides and dropped to his feet behind the wagon. He fell upon a hide man with his knife and plunged it into the man's body. Ransom King brought the Indian down. He swapped ends with his rifle and clubbed another Comanche crawling under a wagon.

Relieved of the pressure at the ends of the line, men came hurrying back to bolster up the middle. Withering fire began throwing the Indians back. Jameson raised up to fire a shot.

Suddenly a bullet struck him with the force of a sledge. He fell back, dropping his rifle, grabbing at his left shoulder. Celia was instantly at his side, desperately seeking the wound.

"Look out," Jameson cried. "Another one."

She whirled and grabbed up the rifle he had dropped. "It's Kills His Enemies," she breathed. She raised the heavy barrel, propped it against a wagon bed. The painted Comanche came streaking in, his war bonnet strung out in the wind behind him. He saw her and raised his lance, screaming.

The rifle belched fire. Kills His Enemies fell back, a gaping hole in the streak of red paint that crossed his chest. He rolled over in the muddy grass and lay still. Then only the war bonnet moved, the feathers still fluttering in the wind.

The gunfire slowed and finally dwindled to silence.

Celia Westerman knelt over Jameson and began to work his coat off his left shoulder. "They're gone," she said gravely. "I don't think they'll be back, not after all this."

The retreating Indians were almost out of sight now. Behind them they left a bloody battlefield strewn with fallen horses and fallen men. There would be wailing in the lodges tonight, Jameson thought grimly.

Celia tore away Jameson's shirt. He grimaced, clenching his teeth to keep from crying out. "It went through," she said. She pulled her shirt-tail out of the trousers Pruitt had given her and tore off a large piece of it to stanch the bleeding.

Jameson lay back weakly, trying to hold himself firm, trying to keep the sky from starting to spin. His head ached unmercifully.

"What about the others? How many casualties?"

Shad Blankenship and Reb Pruitt came up in a moment. "We got three dead. One of them's Ludlow," Shad said. "Several wounded. They can all walk but one. He may not live. Arrows brought down six or eight mules we may have to shoot."

Jameson nodded weakly. "All right. Let's move, quick as we can."

They buried the three dead men a few yards from the creek bank, carefully moving the sod back, then replacing it to hide the grave. Sitting down, Jameson read over them from the old Bible he always carried. He felt a deep touch of sorrow, especially at the loss of Ludlow. The brooding, dark-bearded hide handler had been one of the best, when the time came.

Celia bandaged Jameson's shoulder and bound it tightly. The crew harnessed the mules and hitched them to the wagons. In a while they had them strung out, ready.

Jameson tried to stand, but he could not. He leaned weakly against a wagon, Celia holding his arm. "All right, Shad, let's get them rolling."

Shad moved away. Ransom King stood there, and Trencher. It suddenly occured to Jameson that almost everyone was there. Trencher held a shotgun in his hand. Jameson's shotgun. He was glaring at King.

"You gonna tell him, King, or do I have to?"

They had been arguing. King said, "It's not the time."

"For what?" Jameson demanded weakly. "Time for what?"

"Time to tell you you're stayin' here," Trencher declared. "We're takin' your wagons!"

16

JAMESON FELT his knees give way as the meaning soaked through his drumming brain. He held harder to the wagon.

"King," he said tightly, "I can't believe it."

In a rough voice Trencher said, "You can believe it, Jameson. We had it hatched out before we ever left Dodge. He was ready to call it off after you helped us out of that fight yesterday. But *I'm* not ready. And I'm not goin' to be."

King looked half defiant, half sour. "Sorry, Jameson. It looked like a good idea at the time. I didn't know I was really going to get to like you."

Jameson looked angrily down the line of hide wagons. "But you like money better."

King smiled wryly. "These hides, the wagons and mules will fetch a fancy price. I'll be able to clear out of this country and never have to look at a stinking buffalo again."

"The minute you set foot in Dodge they'll have you. They haven't forgotten these wagons."

"We won't go to Dodge. There are places west of Dodge, like Granada, where they buy hides and mules and wagons. Then I'll fade away, Jameson. I won't be seen again."

In the grinding of futile anger, Jameson's hand clenched the rim of a wagon wheel. Realization came to him. "You've been a hide thief all along, haven't you, King? I'll bet even these wagons you got for me were stolen. That's how you were in with Budge. That's why he didn't fit the part."

He looked at the men. They were backing King now. He knew he had no one left but Shad Blankenship and Reb Pruitt. Pruitt wouldn't be any help. One of the men held a gun on him.

And Shad . . .where was Shad?

Celia was pleading with King. "You can't leave him here, wounded like this. He'll die."

Trencher grinned viciously. "Who you think it was put that bullet in him? It wasn't no Injun. I just didn't make as good a shot as I aimed to."

King glanced quickly at Trencher. "You didn't. . . ."

"I did."

King's face darkened as he glared at Trencher. Then he turned back to Jameson. "I didn't plan on that. But it can't alter things now. We've got to leave you—you see that, can't you, Jameson?"

Fury welled in Jameson, fury that gave him a sudden strength. He stood clear of the wagon, swaying a little.

"I see you'd better kill me now, King, because if I *do* get out of this I'll hunt you down. I'll find you if it takes years. You can't go far enough to get away from me."

Trencher leveled his shotgun. King struck it down.

Trencher said angrily, "You heard what he said."

King nodded with grimness. "But he *won't* find me, Trencher. We're leaving him alive, like we agreed."

Then Shad Blankenship's voice cracked like a whip. "Put them guns down, King!"

Shad stepped from behind a wagon, his big Sharps in his hand. Surprise in his face, then dismay, King dropped his gun. Trencher made a motion as if to lay the shotgun down. Suddenly the muzzle tilted upward and spat flame. Shad jerked back, slamming against the wagon. His rifle slipped from his fingers. He crumpled.

"Shad!" Jameson cried. He lurched toward the old man and fell to his knees beside him. "Shad!"

But Shad Blankenship had lived out his days. Now he was gone . . . gone the way of the other mountain men.

Jameson arose, fury ridging his paled face. He made a grab for Shad's rifle but never touched it. Something struck him across the back of the head. There was a burst of fire in his brain, and he pitched forward into darkness. . . .

"Gage!" Celia Westerman's voice broke in anguish. King grabbed her arm. She whirled back to fight him. In sharp impatience he brought up his fist and sent her sprawling.

"Blast you," he exclaimed, "I never wanted you here in the first place. I knew you'd get in the way when the time came. I've got a good mind to leave you here with him. But I won't."

He turned to one of the men behind him. "Pitch her in the wagon yonder."

Then he faced the other men, his fists knotted. "Anybody changed his mind and want to stay here?" No one moved. He glared at Reb Pruitt. "You weren't in on it, Pruitt, but you can be. Which had you rather do, stay here with Jameson or go on with us?"

Pruitt looked at Jameson, lying unconscious across Shad Blankenship's body. Then he glanced at the wagon where Trencher and another man had carried Celia Westerman. He chewed his lip, studying hard.

"I reckon I'll go," he said.

Consciousness was slow in coming back to Gage Jameson. The wound had drawn him down even more than the blow on the head. He raised up on his good elbow and heard whimpering. A hairy body touched him. It was Shad Blankenship's old black dog.

"Easy, Ripper," Jameson said softly. "Easy."

He sat up, his head seeming to whirl around and around, throbbing unmercifully. He blinked until his sight cleared. The black dog nuzzled him and whimpered again.

Jameson turned painfully and looked down at Shad's slack body. He turned the old man over onto his back and stared into the wrinkled face until the tears welled hot and stinging into his eyes. Tenderly he picked the caked mud from the rusty beard and smoothed it out.

"Shad," he whispered, his throat so tight it felt as if a knife blade were cutting into it. "Shad, you shouldn't have tried it."

The black dog nuzzled Blankenship's face, whimpering. Jameson reached across and patted Ripper on the head. "Both of us, boy," he said. "Both of us."

He looked about him then. The wagons were gone. He had no way of knowing how long it had been. An hour anyway, perhaps two. He tried to push to his feet and fell back. The second time he made it. He stood there swaying until some strength returned to him.

The dead Indians and horses still lay where they had fallen in that last wild charge.

Jameson knew the Comanches wouldn't leave these dead out here to rot. They would be back for them. And if they found him here . . .

"They didn't leave us anything, did they, boy?" he spoke to the dog. "No gun, no food, nothing." His hand dropped to his belt. They had taken his pistol. And he had lost his knife in the flood.

"Lot of good it'd do me if I had one," he commented painfully. "I couldn't catch a turtle."

Even his hat had blown away, probably down into the creek. So had Shad's.

Shad. Jameson knelt beside the old man again. He couldn't just leave him here. He knew what vengeance Indians sometimes took on a dead body. Revulsion rose in him at the thought of leaving Shad here for that kind of treatment.

He couldn't bury him. He had nothing to dig with, even if he had the strength.

He listened to the roar of the creek. It was falling now, but it still carried a lot of force.

Jameson caught Shad's arm with his good hand

and began to drag. He got him four or five feet the first time before he gave out and had to sit down to rest. The next time he got him to the edge of the cave-off. After resting again, he eased Shad's body down the steep bank and finally got it to the edge of the creek.

"It's a long way from a Christian burial, Shad," he said regretfully. "But it's better than the Comanches would do."

He took Shad's knife and stuck it in his own belt. He pulled Shad out into the creek, wading as far as he could hold up against the current. Then he gave the old man a hard push, out where the current would pick him up and carry him away.

Perhaps down there somewhere the creek would find Shad a grave in the deep sand. He remembered what Shad had said:

"The only hope I got is that when my time comes I can die out here, and be buried where I can listen to the wind blow and the wolves howl."

He watched Shad disappear, and a terrible loneliness swept over him. For more than half of his life, Shad Blankenship had been his teacher, his guide. He had been even more than that—a father.

Now he was gone.

Yet Jameson realized that Shad had outlived his time, that he had dreaded this new, unknown world that would come as the frontier faded. Maybe he would have wanted it this way. Maybe it was meant to be.

Jameson waded out of the creek and reached down to touch the shaggy black dog. "Come on, Ripper. It's you and me now."

He climbed up the creek bank, having to stop

and sit awhile because of the shock of blinding pain. Setting out to follow the deep wagon ruts, he could feel the fever building in him. He ached until he was numb. His legs cried out for him to stop, to fall down and rest. But now he had a job to do, and he kept walking, his feet dragging heavily in the mud.

On the battlefield lay Indian guns and knives and lances, weapons he might have used. But the fever was numbing his brain now. All he could do was keep moving. All he could think of was to get Ransom King.

"Get some sense, King; take it easy," Trencher said irritably. "It's dark already, and you been drivin' these mules like the devil was after you. You'll kill them all if you ain't careful."

Ransom King turned nervously in the saddle and looked toward the wagons. Because of darkness he could see only those closest behind him. Grudgingly he said, "All right, then, let's make camp."

"About time," Trencher grumbled, and turned back to bring up the rear wagons.

"Swing into a circle, Pruitt," King said sharply. "You know how."

Pruitt never nodded, never answered. But he swung the chuck wagon around in his accustomed manner. Without a word he dug a pit and began to build a fire.

"Damn you," King exploded, "put that out!"

"We can't cook without a fire."

"We'll eat it cold."

Chilled, hungry, worn out after losing a night's

sleep, going through the battle, then driving the wagons hard far into darkness, the men grumbled about not having a hot supper. Most of all they missed the coffee. But King would not relent.

They ate cold biscuits, as far as they went, and jerky. Then wearily the men began hauling down their bedrolls.

"Double guard tonight," King said.

Groaning, one of the skinners commented, "Man, we need sleep. After today we ain't fixin' to have any more Injun trouble."

King swung his fist and knocked the man to the ground. "I said double guard. I'll shoot the next man who opens his mouth!"

Even after the guards were posted, King stood in the darkness at the edge of camp, peering intently out into the black, straining to hear.

Trencher came up behind him. "Forget it, King. He won't be comin'."

King turned quickly. "What do you mean?"

"I know what's eatin' you. Been eatin' you all day. You think Jameson will be after us. What you think he is, some kind of devil? He's dead by now. If that wound didn't kill him, the Injuns have. Now forget it."

King clenched his fists. "Maybe he's dead and maybe he isn't. If he isn't, he'll be after us."

Trencher grunted and looked back into camp, where Reb Pruitt was putting up a tent for Celia Westerman. "It ain't Jameson that worries me. It's them two."

He drew his knife and tested the cutting edge with his thick finger. "We ought to have left that woman with Jameson. We got to do somethin' about her before we get anywhere near the hide camps or they'll string us up. What do you say I walk her out into the dark a little ways, her and that cook both? It's got to be done, sooner or later.''

King shook his head. ''The men won't stand for killing her,'' he said. ''We've got to figure something.''

Disgustedly Trencher spat. ''She's gettin' to you, that's what's the matter.''

Sharply King responded, ''You're getting too big for your britches, Trencher. I'm still the boss here, and don't forget it.''

Trencher straightened, angrily holding his ground. ''She's yours then, for now. Do what you want to. But before we get to the hide camps, we got to get rid of her.''

17

THE SECOND DAY Jameson knew he was losing his mind. The sun hammered down from a cloudless sky, steam rose from the damp ground and wrapped the heat around him like some angry fiend. Long ago he had ceased to feel hunger, but the torture of thirst continued. His mouth was locked open, his lips dried and cracked, his tongue swollen and afire from the fever that burned in him. The little potholes of water had all dried out.

A maddening ache drummed in his bare head, and through his whole body. Soon now even his sight would be gone. He could see only the wavering image of the prairie ahead of him, dancing and shimmering, an endless reach of grass . . . grass . . . grass like the pitch and roll of the boundless sea.

Long ago he had strayed away from the wagon ruts, away from the creek. He dragged his heavy boots, knowing within reason that he was weaving aimlessly. He knew that soon he would fall to his knees again as he had done so many times already—that next time perhaps he would be unable to rise and would lie here forever in the short grass of the buffalo plains.

He had no idea now where he was going, little hope any more of getting there. The grass looked soft and cool, and he longed to lie down and give it up . . . lie down and sleep and never waken again.

But a single stubborn thread of will remained, and he kept going . . . going . . . going until his mind in its torture seemed to sink back into sleep, and only his legs still moved.

At his side the black dog walked, stopping when Jameson stopped, licking Jameson's face when Jameson fell. Staggering along on the brink of unconsciousness, Jameson tried to force his mind to work. He knew the dangers he faced. At any time now Indians might ride up over the horizon. He wouldn't see them, he knew. Maybe he wouldn't even feel it. Maybe it would be the merciful thing.

Or if it wasn't Indians, it might be a blue norther, with its frigid winds that could cut down even a strong man caught out here in the open. This was early December, and here on these high Texas plains the temperature might plunge murderously fifty or sixty degrees.

Yet somehow he hardly cared. Only two thoughts kept him moving—the need to find Celia Westerman, and his hatred of Trencher and King.

Unable to see, he felt himself suddenly lurching down an incline. His feet went out from under him. He pitched forward on his face—into water.

Water. His fevered body cried out for water. His mouth and throat were leather-dry.

But somehow within him a single sentry of alarm

still watched. Go easy, it told him. Go easy, for the first taste of water may leave you unconscious. You may fall into it and drown, unable to help yourself.

He pulled back, cupping his good hand and lifting a few drops of water to his fever-parched lips, holding himself back by firm will. At the taste of the water he lapsed into darkness.

After awhile he came to again, now stronger than he had been. He felt the dog nuzzling him, licking his face. Once more Jameson cupped his hand and drank slowly, cautiously. He sat on the edge of the waterhole a long time, then, feeling the strength slowly return. Cool water drove the fever back. His sight gradually cleared. In time he was able to regain his feet.

Thirst quenched, Ripper began to nose around in the grass for food. Presently he jumped a rabbit that had come up out of its burrow. He ran the rabbit down and brought it in his mouth, its stout hind legs still kicking.

Hunger had come back to Jameson as the fever had diminished. He took the rabbit from Ripper's jaws and slammed its head against the ground to complete the kill. He skinned and gutted the little animal awkwardly, having only one hand to work with. While Ripper worried the castoff parts, Jameson dug in his pockets and found dry matches. He felt of the grass. Away from the waterhole, the sun had dried it again so that it would burn. He found many buffalo chips there, but they were still wet from the rain and of no use as fuel.

He pulled up dry grass and twisted it as tightly as

he could, setting some of it afire, feeding grass twists into the flame and holding the rabbit over them on the point of the knife.

Ravenously hungry, he was unable to hold himself back long. He began to tear the rabbit apart and wolf it down half cooked.

It wasn't enough, but it partially satisfied his hunger and added to his growing strength. He lay down to rest awhile, knowing he had to get moving soon, had to find that wagon trail. It must be to the west of him, for he knew he had not crossed the creek. He could only have strayed eastward.

Sleep settled over him. Sometime much later he awakened, hearing Ripper growl. He pushed up quickly with his good arm, ice in the pit of his stomach. He knew without looking.

Indians.

Cautiously he pushed to his knees and peered out over the rim of the waterhole. Yonder, still hundreds of yards away, came a lone rider. But it might as well have been a thousand of them, for Jameson had no defense except the knife. And with his wounded shoulder, that would do him little good.

To his right was a little hummock. Keeping low, Jameson crawled behind it and lay still, the ripping knife gripped tightly in his hand, his heart thumping rapidly.

It was a single Comanche warrior, perhaps out scouting for buffalo. He carried a rifle instead of a bow, and a white man's leather cartridge belt instead of an arrow quiver. One feather was fastened in his straight black hair. There was no paint on his round, hard-boned face.

The Indian came straight for the waterhole, knowing where it was. He rode over the rim of it and dropped his leather reins, lifting his left leg over the horse's neck and slipping off to the ground to stretch. He went to his knees to drink of the water. Then his gaze touched the burned grass and scattering of rabbit bones. He turned suspiciously, eyes darting, rifle lifting in his hand.

Cornered, Jameson thought in despair. But he had one chance.

"Sic him, Ripper!" he shouted at the growling black dog. Ripper bounded over the hummock and dove straight at the Comanche's throat. Caught by surprise, the Indian went down under the hurtling weight of the big dog. Ferociously Ripper tore into him, fighting to reach the Indian's throat. Unable to straighten and fire the rifle, the Comanche desperately tried to club the dog with it.

Jameson moved in with the knife. He raised it quickly, and brought it down.

Later he patted the dog's black head. Ripper continued to grumble, hide still rippling with nervousness.

"Good boy," Jameson said quietly. "Now we've got a horse and a rifle. Now we can travel."

With his bad shoulder he had a hard time mounting bareback. Pain knifed through him, and once he thought he had broken the wound open. But finally he managed to get on the horse. His good right hand holding the rifle and the raw-hide reins, he pulled the mount around and headed him west.

Ransom King tipped the bottle up and drank long and hard.

Resentment burned in him as he looked at the men scattered about in their blankets. Rebellion, that was it. The badly wounded Crosson had died late in the afternoon. The men had halted the wagons at dusk, ignoring King's orders to keep them moving. Silently they had buried Crosson, their eyes flashing anger at King for not stopping to ease the dying man's pain. They had built a fire, and Reb Pruitt had cooked them a hot supper. Now King had ordered another double guard and no one had paid him any attention. The men had dropped wearily into their blankets, worn out by the hard drive and loss of sleep. Even Trencher.

King walked to the edge of camp and gazed out into the darkness, wondering about Gage Jameson, wondering at the chill that came to him. Trencher was right. He *had* to be right. Jameson *was* dead. He couldn't have lived this long with that wounded shoulder, with no gun, no food.

Even if alive, he couldn't be following them. He would be holed up somewhere, hiding from Indians, nursing that shoulder and slowly starving to death.

Sure, it was foolish to worry about him. Better for King to spend his time planning how to spend the money he'd get for all these hides, and the stock and wagons. With any luck, he could find a way to avoid having to pay the rest of the crew their share. That, with the rest he had stashed away, would set him up big in Mexico, or in Central America. He could feel the gold in his fingers already. It gave him a warm glow just to think about it.

All his life he had dreamed of pulling off a coup

like this one. Now here it was, safe in his fist.

He raised the bottle again and walked back into the wagon circle. Fools. They hadn't even pulled the wagons up tightly. There was a three-foot gap between the chuck wagon and the next vehicle where a mule could walk right out without scraping a rib.

"Pruitt," he said irritably, finding the cook still up, "plug that gap."

Pruitt made no sign of hearing him. King scowled. They'd have to do something about that cook, sure enough. He sat down against a wagon wheel and looked about camp. Under the wagons men slept exhausted, rolled up in their blankets. Not a man on guard, he'd bet.

Well, he'd stay on guard. He'd stay up all night if he had to. But they'd remember it later. They'd remember it when he got away with all the money.

His eyes drifted then to Celia Westerman's tent. The whisky was warm in his stomach, and he felt a lightheadedness he hadn't allowed himself in a long time. His mind had dwelt on Celia Westerman a lot lately. He hadn't thought of much else but her, and Gage Jameson, and all those wagons loaded with hides.

It wasn't that she was so extra good-looking. In a big town a man wouldn't give her more than a second glance. She didn't have the blood-stirring beauty of a Rose Tremaine, for example. But she *was* a woman, an attractive woman, and she was here.

He sat and pulled on the bottle, staring at her tent. The hunger grew in him. There was no movement about the camp. He took a last drink,

emptying the bottle, and let it drop to the ground
Then he pushed to his feet and walked carefully
toward the tent. The whisky had really gotten to
him now. He found himself weaving.

He ducked to push through the tent flap, finding to
his annoyance that the strings were tied. They
gave way. It was dark inside, but his eyes quickly
adjusted themselves. He could see Celia Wester
man lying in her blankets, awake, watching him

He whispered, "I want to talk to you."

"Get out," she said. "I don't want to hear it."

"They're going to kill you," he said
"Trencher's afraid to leave you alive, to talk."

She made no answer, gave no sign she ever
cared. He could feel her hatred of him like an
electric charge, even though he could not see her
eyes.

He said, "Say the word and I'll get you out of it
We'll go off together, you and me. You'll live like
you've never lived before."

She pushed the blankets aside and stood up. She
was still wearing Reb Pruitt's clothes. "Get out,
told you!"

He grabbed her shoulders. "Listen to me.
want to save you. I'm in love with you, can't you
see that? I want you."

She struck at his face. He grabbed her wrist and
shook her violently.

"Stop it, Celia!"

She fought with him until she lost her footing
She fell backward, and he went down with her
The contact with her body set his pulse to racing
In the darkness, he found her lips and kissed her
roughly, crushing her down.

Too late he saw her hand come up, the wrench in it.

She's been ready for this, he thought, helpless to move away. His brain seemed to explode with the impact. He went down on his elbows. He felt her move away from him, heard the wrench swing again. This time he tumbled forward into darkness.

Celia Westerman paused then, listening, wondering if the struggle had been heard.

She heard nothing. She picked up her coat and began to move toward the front of the tent on her hands and knees.

She stopped abruptly as the tent flap moved. She raised the wrench again, heart in her throat.

Reb Pruitt cautiously poked his head in. He held a six gun, ready. He saw her poised there to strike him, and his eyes widened. His gaze dropped to Ransom King, lying unconscious.

"I ought to've known a Texas girl could handle herself all right," he whispered. "Now come on, and let's get out of here."

Gage Jameson saw the two horsemen as they came down over the rise far ahead of him. Heart quickening, he pulled the Indian pony back from the dried-out wagon ruts and eased down into a hackberry thicket on the creek bank.

"Come on, Ripper," he spoke to the dog. "Get down."

He slid down off the horse and checked the Comanche's old needle gun. It had been stolen out of some Texas home or off some luckless white man after a battle, he figured. The barrel was half

plugged with powder, for Indians knew little abou
taking care of a gun. But it would still fire. Tensin
he went down on one knee and rested the ri
across the other, wondering how he was going
hold it steady with one good hand.

The two riders came into plainer view and h
nervously licked his dry lips. Most of the fever ha
burned itself out, but a little still remained. He sa
that one of the two was leading an extra horse

Suddenly Jameson lowered the rifle and stoc
up, blinking unbelievingly. It couldn't be. But
was!

He walked out, leading the Indian pony, letti
them see him. He saw Reb Pruitt swing a rifle u
then lower it in recognition.

Celia Westerman stepped down from her sadd
and ran to meet him. He quickly moved towa
her. He caught her with his good arm and crush
her to him, dropping his cheek down against th
top of her head, her long blonde hair.

"Gage, Gage," she said softly, holding him
tightly as she could. He could feel the hot tears
her cheek as he brought his hand up to her chi

Reb Pruitt stood there first on one foot, then th
other. Finally he took the sack of grub down fro
Celia's saddle.

"May not be the best time to mention it,"
commented dryly, "but if you're hungry . . ."

Jameson devoured food out of the sack whi
Reb and Celia told him what had happened, ho
they had gotten out of the camp with three saddl
horses, some grub, and several guns.

"I didn't have any hope of findin' you alive
Pruitt admitted. "I tried to talk her into headi

north to find some hide outfit. But she wouldn't have it that way. So we come south, riding in the edge of the creek to keep them from tellin' which direction we went.''

Hunger satisfied, Jameson grimly looked at the guns Reb and Celia had brought. A pistol apiece. A rifle. And his shotgun.

It was the shotgun Trencher had used on Shad. Looking at it, Jameson clenched his fist.

"I'm going to get them," he said tightly. "I've *got* to get them—for Shad."

Reb said, "I don't aim to take up any for King, he don't deserve it. But it was Trencher who shot Shad. It wasn't King."

Jameson said through gritted teeth, "When a man cuts loose a wolf, he's got to answer for whatever that wolf does."

"What're you going to do?" Celia pressed anxiously.

"Going to trail after them. Going to cut the ground out from under King a little at a time. Going to make him sweat while I take everything away from him. And finally, when he's lost everything, I'm going to ride in there and get him. Get him for Shad Blankenship."

18

JAMESON AND PRUITT sat their horses on a sma‹
promontory and gazed down at the hide wagon‹
strung out like a long snake far below them.

"Still pushing hard," Jameson said. "Been lik‹
that every day, daylight to well after dark. Wond‹
he hasn't killed half the stock by now."

Reb Pruitt nodded. "And half the men, to‹
Stirred up as they were when we got out of ther‹
I'm surprised they haven't run off and left hin
Somethin' was eatin' at him pretty bad. I thin
maybe he sensed that you were following aft‹
him."

Jameson swung down from the saddle to re
awhile, never taking his eyes from the wagons. H
left shoulder was stiff and sore, but the fever w‹
several days gone now. He had lost much weigh
Still, his strength had returned, for the most par

His beard was a week or more long, black ar
wiry. His clothes were crusted with mud and dir
He was still bare-headed.

"Not over a couple of days' ride now to the Arkansas," he estimated. "They're going to be jumpy as cats down there, afraid you and Celia went after help and will be bringing a hanging party down on them."

"You think they might run if we was to prod them a little?"

Jameson shrugged. "I don't know. But we're fixing to find out."

At nightfall the three of them moved in toward Ransom King's camp. Working up close while Celia stayed back and held the horses, the two men watched the teamsters circle the wagons and drive the stock inside. Ransom King rode up and down the outside, shouting orders with a fury born of desperation.

"I'll bet he ain't caught much sleep since we been gone," Reb whispered. "Nor let anybody else get much, either."

They stayed out there until the camp quieted down. Then they moved up close to seek out the guards. Satisfied, they crept back out to Celia.

Jameson asked, "Reb, do you think you could move that chuck wagon a few feet, with that horse and your rope?"

Pruitt nodded. "I reckon. Wagon's not heavy loaded any more."

"Then you're going to open a hole in that wagon circle. And I'm going to run out all the horses and mules I can."

They remounted their horses. Celia walked up and pressed against Jameson's leg. "Don't take chances, Gage. Be careful."

"We won't crowd our luck too much," he promised.

Moving their horses in a walk, they worked
carefully up toward the wagons, the black dog
trotting at their heels. They split, Jameson riding
far around the circle and coming in toward a spot
where he had seen no guard. On the other side,
Pruitt was moving in at the chuck wagon.

Jameson halted near the wagons, looking for a
hole where he might put the horse through, listening for Pruitt's rope to sing. But it was silent.

Suddenly he heard the creak of the chuck wagon
as a horse lunged against a rope. He saw the wagon
lurch, then wheel out, leaving a gap in the circle.

Six-gun in hand, Jameson fired into the air and
yelled. Horses and mules within the enclosure
began to mill and stomp. Then, seeing the opening,
they broke out, running. Jameson kept shouting
and firing until he saw men rushing toward him. He
started to spur away.

Then he recognized the bulky man who came in
the lead. He heard the man's roar, saw the gun in
the man's hand.

Instead of running away, Jameson touched
spurs to the horse and headed straight toward the
man. It was Trencher. He saw the spurt of flame
from Trencher's gun, felt the heat as the bullet cut
by his ear. He brought his own six-shooter down
level and squeezed the trigger. He saw Trencher
stagger back, and he fired again.

That, he thought, is for Shad.

He pulled aside as the other men began firing at
him. He leaned low and pushed the horse into a
lope. He circled around and met Reb Pruitt riding
away, driving a sizable string of horses and mules.

The black dog was running too, barking at the animals' heels.

"We got maybe half of them," Reb shouted, "before they cut them off."

Half of them. Jameson felt a glow of triumph. That would hit King where it hurt the most.

"Let's keep them running," he said.

He half expected pursuit, but it didn't come. Next morning they moved in cautiously and found the train already pulled out. Six wagons loaded with hides sat there, deserted for lack of mules to pull them.

"This," Jameson said, "is what will kill King, having to leave these hides."

They found Trencher lying unburied, just where Jameson had left him. They had all hated Trencher.

All day they trailed along well behind King's wagon train, pushing with them the horses and mules they had captured last night. Along in midafternoon they came up over a rise and saw a pair of wagons sitting there. Two men had a wheel off the tongue wagon.

"King must be getting panicky," Jameson commented. "Went off and left them." He checked his six-shooter and looked across at Reb Pruitt. "Want to take them?"

Pruitt nodded.

Jameson said, "You stay back with the stock, Celia."

They moved into a lope. They were almost upon the wagons before the men saw them. One man made a run for a rifle propped up against a wagon wheel. Jameson fired a pop shot at him. Dust puffed under the man's feet. He stopped abruptly and raised his hands.

The other man stood limply, his face drained of color.

"Jameson," he breathed. "I told them it was you last night. You and that black devil of a dog. I told King and he knocked me down. He said it was Indians. Said he'd kill the man who mentioned your name again."

Reb Pruitt grinned through his scraggly growth of beard. "Panicky, Gage, like I told you."

Jameson nodded and frowned at the two men.

"What should we do with them, Reb, shoot them right here?"

The two began to tremble. One pleaded, "Look, Jameson, we didn't know how it was going to turn out. We didn't expect any killing. They said all they were going to do was set you afoot."

Jameson scowled at them. "We ought to shoot you, but we'll give you a chance. Start hiking. If you're ever seen in this country again, you'll hang."

Reb Pruitt unhitched the mules while Jameson watched the two walk eastward out across the prairie, no rifles, no bedding, just a canteen of water from under the wagon seat and the knives in their belts.

Jameson frowned. "It'll give King some more to think about when these two wagons don't come in tonight. Eight wagonloads he's already had to leave behind him. That's half of them, Reb."

They watched from afar as Ransom King made camp. There weren't enough wagons left now to

236

circle. Instead, King left them strung out and tied the remaining animals on picket lines, the lines secured to the wagon wheels.

"Won't be anybody asleep down there to-night," Jameson guessed. "He'll keep them awake, watching the stock."

No fire was built in King's camp that night. For awhile Jameson considered working down there and trying to cut some of the picket lines. But he knew they would be closely watched. It wouldn't be worth the risk.

"We'll worry them a little, just the same," he said. Taking the needle gun, he fired a shot down toward the camp. He heard a burst of shouts and the squeals of animals, then a pounding of hoofs leading off away from camp.

"There went a picket line," Pruitt laughed.

Jameson lay down on the ground to rest awhile, his eyes on Celia Westerman. He felt a stirring of pride at the way she had taken all this, the help she had been.

Occasionally during the night he would get up and move around, looking off toward King's camp. At the back of his mind lurked a worry that the men might come out looking for him. But he doubted, really, that they would. They couldn't know for sure who was stalking them, or how many.

Reb Pruitt shook him awake at daylight. "Gage, there's somethin' goin' on down there."

Jameson arose, pausing to smile at the sight of Celia Westerman still lying asleep beneath a blanket that they had taken out of one of the hide wagons yesterday.

Reb pointed. "What do you make of it?"

The hide men were knotted up together in a group, facing one man. That man could only be Ransom King. Jameson wasn't sure, but he thought King held a rifle.

He watched King gesturing angrily. The men milled back and forth, and occasionally some of them used their hands in violent argument. King raised the rifle, leveling it at them.

Someone threw something at King and he stepped aside, off balance. Then the men were on him. Jameson thought he saw a flash, and he heard the delayed report of a gun. The melee ended. The men scattered, catching up horses and mules. They streamed out of camp, heading east, abandoning the wagons.

"They're gettin' away," Pruitt said anxiously.

Jameson shook his head. "Let them go. We wouldn't know what to do with them if we had them, and we know they'll never dare come back. The one we want is still down there."

Only one man remained. He was stretched out on the ground. Watching from afar, Jameson thought for awhile that they had killed him. But presently King stood groggily and staggered to a wagon. He held himself up against a wheel, letting his strength return.

"Want to go down and get him?" Pruitt asked.

"No, let's wait awhile. Let's see what he's going to do. I want to see if he sticks with his wagons or if he gives up and runs."

King wasn't running, yet. Jameson could only imagine the frustration in King's mind as he leaned against the wheel, looking helplessly at the hide wagons strung out there, each pair laden with a thousand dollars and more in flint hides. All this he had held in his grasp. Now it had slipped through his fingers.

It was still there, its very presence a mockery of his extravagant dreams, his well-developed plans.

The hides were there within his reach, but worthless to him now because he could not move them.

This was what Jameson had been waiting for, to let the ground slip away from under King's feet and leave him with nothing but the gray ashes, the dark knowledge of defeat.

"We better get him, Gage, before he runs."

"He won't run," Jameson told Pruitt, "not so long as he thinks he can salvage a little of it."

Four mules remained on one picket line. King harnessed them one by one and hitched them to a pair of wagons. He popped the whip, and the mules strained so that the muscles bulged on their chests and on their legs. The wagons moved, but slowly. The mules would wear out before they had gone a mile. It was too heavy a load.

King pulled them up and sat there, looking back dejectedly at the wagons he was leaving. Finally he climbed down and unhitched the trail wagon, leaving it there with the rest.

All he had now was the tongue wagon, with no more than three or four hundred hides. Only this, where once he had had fifteen wagons, every one loaded.

"Like the dregs at the bottom of the cup," Jameson thought aloud.

King cracked the whip again. The mules

strained, and the wagon rolled out.

Jameson watched him awhile, then rose to his feet. "Let me have that shotgun, Reb. I think it's time now."

Celia Westerman pushed back the blanket and got to her feet. "Gage, what are you going to do?"

"I'm going to get Ransom King."

Dismayed, she looked at the shotgun. "With that?"

"It's what they used on Shad."

Celia caught his arm. "Gage, please let the law handle him. Take him alive. Take him in."

He looked at Pruitt. "Let me have a couple of extra shells."

Reluctantly Reb handed them to him. "You ought to listen to her, Gage."

Celia pleaded. "You're not a killer, Gage. Don't make yourself one by doing this. You'll have it with you as long as you live."

But Gage Jameson could still see Shad Blankenship's broken body the way they had left it there on the prairie. That Trencher had paid for it wasn't enough. There was still the man who had cut loose the wolf.

He leaned down and kissed Celia. "Wait for me," he said. "I'll be back."

He rode out, paralleling King's wagon.

Later he could see a brushy creek far ahead, cutting diagonally across his path. He knew King would have to move over it. That would be the time to get him, while he had his hands full in crossing the stream.

For Jameson's shoulder was still stiff. He had only one hand with which to handle the gun. He had to take all the advantage he could get.

He rode on in an easy lope, splashing into the creek, pushing across and reining up on the far side. The water had been deeper than he thought, two and a half or three feet. Staying in the brush, he watched impatiently for King's wagon.

And at last it came.

King angled his mules toward an open spot on the brushy bank. There was a two-foot drop-off into the water. King hauled the mules up to a slow walk, easing them out into the creek slowly so the wheels would take the drop without breaking spokes or coupling pole.

Watching him from the cover of brush, Jameson felt his heart pound.

It's time, he thought.

Shotgun ready, he pushed his horse into the water with a splash. King reined up suddenly, whip in his hand, the front wheels of the wagon just starting to slide down the drop.

He stared at Jameson openmouthed, his face blanching. "I guess I knew it was you all the time," he said in resignation.

Jameson gripped the shotgun. "You're going to die, King. Die the way Shad did."

King's voice lifted. "*I* didn't kill him, Gage. It was Trencher."

Jameson's voice crackled with fury.

"You planned the whole thing. You set it up. You got Shad killed just as much as if you had pulled the trigger."

Moving out into the creek, closer to King, he lifted the shotgun.

"Gage," King exclaimed, "I haven't got a gun.

Honest to God, they took them away from me.
They left me unarmed."

Jameson hesitated, wondering if King might be
lying. Somehow, he knew he wasn't. And he knew
he couldn't shoot King down in cold blood.

Instead of feeling cheated, he felt a vague sense
of relief.

"Then I'll take you in," he said at last, lowering
the shotgun. "But you know what they'll do,
King. They'll hang you!"

King sat motionless on the wagon seat, his eyes
sick at the contemplation of such a death.

"That," he said in a strained voice, "is no way
for a man to die."

Suddenly his arm moved. He lifted the whip.

Before Jameson could bring the shotgun up
again, the searing whip wrapped around him. His
horse reared and plunged in panic. Grabbing at the
horn with his one good hand, Jameson accidently
fired the shotgun into the air. The kick of it set him
off balance. He tumbled from the saddle into the
cold water.

In desperation King hauled his mules around,
trying to turn. But the front wheels slipped in the
mud, and the right hind wheel skidded from the
drop-off. The wagon tilted. For a moment it stood
balanced precariously on two wheels while Ransom King struggled to keep his seat.

He slipped off and fell into the muddy creek. An
instant later the wagon tipped over and crashed
down on its side in a huge splash of water. It lay
there then in the brown stir of mud, the left rear
wheel spinning.

King never came up.

Jameson waded hurriedly to the wagon. He couldn't see for the mud. He dropped down under the cold water, feeling around for King. He caught King's hand, felt the man threshing wildly, pinned beneath the load of hides.

Jameson braced himself and pulled hard with his one good hand. He felt the hides shift just a little, but not enough. He pulled desperately, feeling King's struggle growing weaker. He pulled until the world went black before his eyes. But his own strength had been drained by the wound in his shoulder.

He heard horses running. He saw Reb Pruitt and Celia galloping up to the creek.

"Reb," he called in desperation, "come help me! Come quick!"

By the time Reb got there, King was limp. With Reb's help Jameson pulled him out from under the heavy hides. They dragged him to the bank. But it was no use.

"Too late," Reb Pruitt said quietly.

Jameson knelt, breathing heavily. "If it hadn't been for this shoulder . . ."

Regret touched him then, and he said evenly, "There was a lot that was likable about him. If he'd been honest. . . What gets into a man like that, Reb? What is it that sets him wrong?"

Reb Pruitt shook his head, looking at the overturned wagon in the creek, then at the lifeless body of Ransom King.

"Who can say, Gage? Stolen hides, stolen wagon. Only one man to help him, and that man crippled because of what King himself had done. Strange, ain't it, the way a man's life catches up with him?"

Celia took Jameson's hand. "I'm glad *you* didn't have to do it, Gage."

He nodded solemnly. "So am I. I wanted to, but now I'm glad I didn't."

He looked northward then. "Somewhere up yonder, past the Arkansas, we ought to be able to find some buffalo hunters out of luck and looking for something to do. We'll bring them and get the stock and wagons."

Reb said, "You'll have King's wagons, too. I reckon you've earned them."

Jameson shook his head, thinking of Nathan Messick, and the sister who was left with no one to provide for her. "I don't want them," he said. "But I know where they'll do some good."

Looking southward again he said, "Someday we'll go back to Texas together, Reb, you and Celia and me. And we'll stay there."

"That'll be a good day for all of us," Reb replied. Then he turned back to figure a way of getting the overturned wagon out of the creek.

★★★★★★★★★★★★★★★★★★★★★★

The Biggest, Boldest, Fastest-Selling Titles in Western Adventure!

★★★★★★★★★★★★★★★★★★★★★★

CHARTER'S MOST WANTED LIST

Nelson Nye

__14263-X	DEATH VALLEY SLIM	$2.75
__48925-7	LONG RUN	$2.50
__80611-2	THIEF RIVER	$2.50

Giles A. Lutz

__34286-8	THE HONYOCKER	$2.50
__06682-8	THE BLACK DAY	$2.50

Will C. Knott

__29758-7	THE GOLDEN MOUNTAIN	$2.25
__71146-4	RED SKIES OVER WYOMING	$2.25

Benjamin Capps

__74920-8	SAM CHANCE	$2.50
__82139-1	THE TRAIL TO OGALLALA	$2.50